A Year
And A Day

Patsy Collins

For Mum.

With thanks and love.

Chapter One

Stella tried to ignore the aroma from the hotdog stand as she bounced along in time to the rock music blaring from the dodgems.

"Step away from the burgers, mate." Daphne attempted to steer her back into the hot, noisy heart of the funfair.

"It was hotdogs, not burgers and I'm hungry."

"You're as bad as the kids I cook for, always wanting to eat junk food rather than wait for a proper meal. I'm sure you'll survive until we get back to my place for a curry."

Stella could hardly make out her friends words but the thought of the crispy lamb samosas, creamy chicken korma and fragrant pilau rice Stella intended to order revived her enough for her to follow her friend to the next stall. Giant playing cards were arranged on a cork board and 'all' they had to do to win was to land a dart on three which matched.

Daphne threw first, if you could call her pathetic efforts throwing.

"Imagine you're throwing them at someone you don't like," Stella advised. "And put some effort into it."

Daphne threw again.

"Better."

"I was thinking of you."

"Were not! Come on, let me show you how it's done."

Stella conjured up the mental image of a short, smug policeman and aimed. One, two, three darts into each seven of diamonds.

"Lucky little lady here just won our top prize," the stall holder bellowed for the benefit of passing potential customers. "What'll you have, love?"

Stella selected a huge panther, with fur as dark and glossy as her own hair.

"Good choice; black cats are lucky. Maybe we'll pull tonight," Daphne said.

"Only thing I'm going to pull is a muscle carrying this thing around and it won't be lucky if I have to pay extra on the rides for him. Still, I think we've been on the best ones already."

"You're probably right. Let's just wander around for a bit."

They'd already done quite a lot of wandering and Stella was getting the distinct impression it wasn't entirely aimless. She narrowed her eyes at Daphne, but to no effect.

"I was thinking... shall we get our fortunes told?" Daphne suggested, twisting her blonde hair around one finger.

She sounded as though she'd just thought of the idea. Stella wasn't fooled: she was relieved. She'd suspected Daphne was up to something and worried she'd planned another matchmaking attempt with her brother, John. The last time had been a disaster. OK, it had seemed like a good idea at the time, twelve years, four months and six days ago and Stella was completely over it, but she still didn't want a repeat performance.

"I'll take that as a yes, then," Daphne said.

"Take what as a what?"

"We're going to get our fortunes told."

"No way; it's stupid. Anyway, I'm not sure I want to know what's going to happen."

"Why not?"

"I hate having my life arranged for me, you know that. It's bad enough when other people do it, I don't like the thought that it's all set up in advance and there's nothing I can do to change it. Besides, looking into the past didn't do me much good, did it? Why would seeing the future be any better?"

"Stella, I'm sorry, I didn't think about that. If it will upset you then of course we won't do it." Daphne put her arms around Stella and hugged her.

Stella felt guilty. When she'd turned eighteen and tried unsuccessfully to trace her parents Daphne had been there for her and swore she'd never abandon her friend. The idea of having her fortune told did make Stella uncomfortable, but it was unfair to pretend to be more upset than she really was just to get her own way.

"I'm OK. I just think all this mumbo jumbo is a bit daft."

"Asking for guidance isn't daft," Daphne said. She linked her arm through Stella's and urged her to keep walking over the dust-dry playing field.

"It depends who you ask," Stella said. "Personally I'm not sure a complete stranger wearing a headscarf, who'll have moved on by tomorrow and who's being paid to say what you want to hear, is the best bet."

"Lighten up! I just thought it'd be fun. Anyway, Rosie-Lee is well known. I read an article about her and she's really good. And she offers a money back guarantee." Daphne gestured to the brightly painted caravan and its sign listing the almost famous people whose fortunes had been read by Romany Rosie-Lee. "You'd be able to find her again if you really wanted to."

"Seems we've found her even though I didn't want to."

"Shall we do it then? It'd be a laugh," Daphne said.

Stella sighed.

"Please. I really want to."

Stella knew when to give in gracefully. "OK, OK. My treat." Paying for the reading might help her feel in control of the situation.

"OK, but I'll get the take-away."

"Deal. Just as long as she tells me something nice and we agree it's just a laugh and you absolutely promise not to do anything stupid based on anything she says."

"Deal."

Unspoken between them was the memory of the time the previous year when Daphne had insisted they took the number seven bus because her horoscope had mentioned an exciting journey connected with that number. In fact the seven mile walk home after missing the last one back really had been quite eventful; a thunder storm made their mobiles useless and torrential rain ruined their clothes. Their wet shoes rubbed giving them blisters, which made the walk take even longer. Daphne's parents had become worried and called the police - or rather they'd done something far more embarrassing. They'd called Daphne's policeman brother John, who'd driven out in search of them.

Stella's wet blouse had clung, almost transparently to her top half, her trousers were dragged down with the weight of the water and mascara streaked her face. She'd had to endure watching his shoulders shake with laughter as she sat behind him for the drive home and again when he gave her an umbrella for her birthday soon after.

Then there was the time Daphne had read some mystical mumbo jumbo claiming that for her star sign orange would lead the way. Daphne, without stopping to think, had dyed her hair, plus the bathroom tiles and carpet in Stella's flat in a particularly hideous version of that colour.

Daphne stood outside the gypsy wagon with her hand over her heart. "I promise," said and then gave a Girl Guide salute. It would have been a lot more reassuring if they'd ever got around to joining that organisation.

Daphne went in first. Stella tried waving her stuffed cat about to create a breeze, but the effort just made her hotter still. She held her hair away from her neck and glared at the gaudily painted caravan. If they'd really wanted it to look like an old fashioned wagon, they should have unhitched it from the gleaming Range Rover it was connected to. She looked at her watch yet again. How long could it take to rave over tall, dark handsome strangers and promise Dappy Daphne she'd live happily ever after? Stella hoped that was the sort of thing Rosie-Lee would tell her. What she dreaded was the gypsy promising what she wanted most; a loving family. She couldn't bear to be told that and know it was all a scam, she'd rather keep her dream.

Fun; that's what Daphne had said this was going to be. Compared with the awful thought of a go on the Tunnel of Love with John, being conned out of her cash by a gypsy might be bearable. Not actual fun, just more fun than another lecture from John the cop. Ever since she'd recovered from the humiliation of their break-up, he'd felt he had the right to act as though he was personally responsible for her safety and moral welfare. And ever since then he kept creeping into her thoughts when she really didn't want him to be there.

She most definitely didn't want to think of the time, so long ago, when she'd been pleased to have his company at the fair. She'd climbed out of her foster parents' window and

John had grabbed her waist to help her safely down. He'd taken her and Daphne to the fair, spending all his paper round money on rides and candyfloss for the pair of them. He'd taken her out a few times after that, without Daphne as a chaperone and was the first boy who'd ever kissed her. And then it had all gone horribly wrong and stayed that way.

At last, the door to the gypsy caravan opened and the first part of Stella's ordeal was over.

"You'll never believe what she's told me," Daphne said as she emerged from the caravan and climbed down the antique wood and brushed aluminium steps.

"You're quite right, I'm not going to believe any of it. Oh well, I suppose I'd better get this over with."

The door closed behind Stella with a clunk that sounded unnervingly permanent. There was no need to panic, Daphne was right outside and the woman before her was just an entertainer. Nothing she would say could hurt Stella.

The fortune teller looked the part, Stella admitted that much. The interior of the van was flamboyantly draped in a scarlet velvet cloth embellished with pentangles and signs of the zodiac picked out in gold and purple. In comparison the slim, dark haired woman seemed subtly attired. The colourful scarf could almost pass as a fashion accessory and her gold hooped earrings were more tasteful than bling.

Stella looked down at the crystal ball and just for a moment she imagined she really could see swirling mists in it. Stella pulled back her shoulders and sat upright on her seat. Probably it was just smoke from the incense that was burning. Whatever she'd imagined she'd seen soon cleared and the gypsy said the reading could begin.

The gypsy first gave Stella a pack of cards and invited her to shuffle them.

"Lay five in a row here." The gypsy indicated a silver tray inset with what might have been jewels but were probably coloured glass.

Stella turned over five cards, chosen at random. They were all very pretty, showing flowers and swirly patterns in bright colours. You wouldn't want them as wallpaper, but they'd make lovely table mats.

Rosie-Lee made a great show of studying the cards and nodding her head as though she'd learnt something interesting. "You have a close friend. Closer to you than a family could be."

Stella gasped. No, it was just a guess on the gypsy's part; she knew nothing of Stella's missing family.

"I won't speak of the painful past; that is gone."

Stella nodded. It was gone, the gypsy was right.

"There are happy memories too," Rosie-Lee suggested.

Oh great, this was like listening to the weather forecast. Half of it would be about what had already happened and most of that not always right. The rest would be vague predictions, most of them generalities and hedged bets.

"Aren't you supposed to tell me what's going to happen, not what already has?" Stella tried to soften her comment with a smile; she hadn't meant to snap at Rosie-Lee, she just wanted this to be over as quickly as possible.

"You will soon be going on an exciting journey across the water."

"Well, I was thinking of going to Spain for my holiday," Stella admitted.

"You will meet a tall, dark stranger."

"You forgot about handsome." Stella grinned. This was much more like it. Clichés she could handle.

"Oh, he will be very handsome and you will be instantly attracted," Rosie-Lee confirmed. The woman seemed to be playing along.

"And get married, win the lottery and live happily ever after?"

"You doubt my power, but a year and a day from now you will believe. Your friend, the girl who came in before you, she does not doubt me."

"Who Daphne? Oh no, she believes in it all. Doesn't do a thing 'til she's read her horoscope in the morning. She'll follow any advice you give her to the letter. And all your predictions will come true; she'll make sure they do."

The gypsy's dark eyes looked into hers and Stella felt they saw below the surface. She'd rather hear more about her forthcoming holiday. Maybe the gypsy could suggest a good beach or which colour bikini would suit her?

"Your friendship will be closer still after you save her life," the gypsy gestured to where Daphne waited outside. "Your paths are close. Your long, healthy lives will be forever entwined if you take care of yourself and your friendship."

Rosie-Lee continued to stare, almost hypnotically, into Stella's eyes. She doubted there was much they didn't see. Tearing her gaze away she reminded herself the gypsy probably overheard her reluctantly agree to this and offer to pay for Daphne's fortune to be read, so it wasn't surprising she'd guessed they were close friends.

"I'm not as gullible as I look, you know." Stella tried not to glance at the 'genuine precious stones' bangle she'd won on the hoopla and the furry panther which had cost twice as much to win as it was worth.

"My powers are real. I shall prove it to you. I shall write down what I have said today, and I shall write something more, something that will prove to you I really can see your true path."

"No," Stella whispered. She didn't want to believe her future was mapped out from the moment of her birth. Then she'd been unwanted, alone with no family to turn to. Stella felt tears sting her eyes, then the warmth of the gypsy's hands on her own.

"The future is not the past."

Stella looked up into the smiling face.

"A year and a day from now, you'll willingly believe."

Chapter Two

Stella shook her head, confused. What she'd thought was a threat she'd not get her dream had in fact been a promise that she would. For a moment she almost wished she could believe Rosie-Lee. She couldn't of course, it was all just guesswork despite the sincere sounding voice and soul searching gaze.

"Oh yeah and if you're right what then? Do I have to give you my first born child or something?"

"No. You must promise to tell her the truth."

"Fine. I'd do that anyway, you know."

"So you do believe I can see the future?"

Stella laughed. "OK, you got me there."

The gypsy took Stella's right hand and traced a long, red painted nail over her palm. Next came the flattery and softening up she'd expected. Stella was a strong woman, interesting, complex and well liked. Well, of course she was. She couldn't argue about her inner beauty, or her usually sound judgement of character either and liked the advice to trust her heart and the understanding of her friend.

Stella couldn't fault the woman for putting on a good show. Daphne was right; it had been fun in the end, so was worth the money. She asked for a few more details on her tall, handsome hero before she accepted the purple envelope containing the slip of paper on which the gypsy had written her proof. It smelt of something vaguely familiar she couldn't identify and was decorated with silver crescent moons.

"Come on then, what were you told?" Daphne asked, pouncing on Stella and stroking the panther wedged under her arm.

"Rosie-Lee said that you'd turn into a giant pink frog unless you bought me a take-away and a bottle of wine right now," Stella said.

"OK, I can take a hint. What did she really say?"

The girls walked around the edge of the fair where it was relatively quiet.

"I'm going to meet a tall, dark handsome stranger, journey across water, all the usual stuff. I suppose you got the same?" Stella said.

"No, I didn't. She said that number three would be lucky for me and I need a new job."

"She was right there, Daffs. I expect you flinched or something when she mentioned work. She's probably really good at reading body language, that's her skill."

"Maybe. What else did she tell you?"

"She saw me walking down the aisle with a friend at my side, but she's just saying what she thinks I want to hear and anyway as we're in our mid twenties, it's quite likely we'll get married sometime soon."

"And if you do and don't ask me to be your bridesmaid then I'll be reading your horoscope for you and it won't be pretty."

"Exactly," Stella agreed with a laugh.

They waited for the lights to change so they could cross safely into the High Street.

Daphne said, "Don't worry, you'll be my bridesmaid and I'll be yours. She said that our lives will be entwined and if we look after our health and each other we'll have long healthy lives."

"I got all that too. That's just a combination of overhearing us talking outside the caravan, reading body language and common sense," Stella said.

"If it's all so sensible why can't you accept it?"

"Come on; I'll meet a tall, dark handsome stranger and fall instantly in love. Even you can't expect me to believe that?"

"If he's handsome you might fall for him. And you do have a weakness for tall men."

"Who doesn't? You can't tell me that you're hoping to spend your life with a short, ugly pale bloke."

"I already do, according to you!"

That was true. Daphne currently shared a flat with her brother. John was the total opposite of Stella's idea of a romantic hero. Why she'd let Daphne talk her into believing she fancied him when they'd both been teenagers was a constant mystery. At least it would be if she ever thought of John, which she didn't. Not ever.

Every seat in the blissfully cool Indian restaurant was taken.

"Do you think it's so busy because the food is great or because they've got air conditioning?" Stella asked.

"Lovely isn't it? If there was a spare table I'd be wanting to eat in. Don't worry though, the food's good. I've been here before."

"Am I sensing that your flat is going to be as hot and stuffy as mine?"

"Afraid so, but at least the company is cool."

"Thanks mate," Stella said, fluttering her eye lashes. "So, chicken korma for me. What are you having?" she added before Daphne could point out she'd been referring to herself. Fortunately Daphne was nearly as easily distracted by the mention of food as Stella was herself.

As Stella ordered their take-away food, Daphne sent a text.

"I'm just letting John know we're OK. Since that girl in out street got robbed he's been even more protective than usual," she said as they sank into the plush red seats to wait.

"Tell me about it, he came round my place and checked my door lock was up to scratch," Stella said.

"I told him it was, so you can't blame me for that."

"I don't blame you. Not this time anyway. He did have to admit the lock I'd had put on was OK, but he wasn't happy with the windows and fitted special catches so now they're a right pain to open. Every time I try to get a bit of breeze into the flat I chip a nail."

Daphne paid for the meal. "Rosie-Lee said to try something connected with my senses," she said when she returned to her seat. "For a job I mean, not to attract a man."

"That's not a bad idea. Taste is a sense; what about that new Italian restaurant that's opening near me? Your talents are wasted in the school canteen. It'd be more convenient and you could come to my place for your breaks."

"And you'd get cheap pizza and pasta and act as guinea pig for any dessert recipes I wanted to try?"

"What are friends for?" Stella grinned. She began unwrapping one of the chocolate mints the waiter had added to the saucer he used to return Daphne's credit card.

"Battering to death with a stuffed panther?" Daphne suggested as she took the mint away from Stella. The effect of her words was ruined by her giggle.

"You don't want to do that, Daphne my girl. Apparently I'm going to be saving your life some time soon."

"Aaaw. Thanks, mate."

"Well, you know I would if the need arose; you're like the sister I never had, but you won't need saving. That's just another example of her being a good judge of character and I suppose she must have thought I was the protective type because I said something about you being gullible..."

"You never!"

"Yeah. She didn't need any special gift to see I wasn't falling for her act. She reckoned she could prove it was all true though."

"How?" Daphne asked.

"She's written down what she said will happen for us and something else that she says will make me a believer a year and a day from now. Tell you what, you keep it and we'll read it together in a year's time. That way you'll know I'm not cheating by making sure it doesn't happen," Stella said.

"Right. I'll seal it up so you know I haven't tried to influence you so it does."

"OK, but let's do it properly; you know with a wax seal instead of a bit of sticky tape," Stella said.

"That's a bit dramatic isn't it?"

"No more dramatic than that clearing mists stuff you've just put me through." And wax would be a lot easier to remove and reseal without detection than sticky tape would be.

Stella was glad to put down the panther when they got back to Daphne's flat.

"I'm sure my arms must be a good couple of inches longer."

"He can't be heavier than the curry and wine. I suppose it is a he?" Daphne said as she set plates on the table.

"He is. I bet he is heavier and he's bigger and I have been carrying him for loads longer and I'm weak with hunger."

"I'm working as fast as I can," Daphne said, removing lids from the foil containers. "What are you going to call him?"

"Thirteen."

"Thirteen! You can't; it's unlucky."

"No it's not, it's just a number. Actually in this case it's a date; the thirteenth of July and as I won him today, that makes it lucky. Plus as he's named after a date that means I'll always have a date to snuggle up with."

"OK, you've convinced me." Daphne's expression suggested she was only convinced there was no point arguing, but at least she returned her attention to a far more important issue: curry.

While Daphne unpacked the food and garnished it with chopped coriander. Stella selected a CD from Daphne's collection. They ate the tasty meal and discussed every detail of the fortunes they'd been given. Almost every detail; Stella didn't want to spoil Daphne's enjoyment by mentioning the bit about family sadness. As Rosie-Lee said, it was all in the past.

Once they'd eaten, Stella insisted they do everything properly by listening to The Searchers singing *Love Potion*

Number Nine before lighting a candle, dimming the lights, laying the envelope face down on the table and pouring more wine.

Daphne proposed a toast. "To the future."

"The future," Stella agreed. She sipped her wine. "It's looking Rosé-er already."

"That's dreadful. Just for that, I'm going to make you use one of my lucky charms for the seal." Daphne waved her festooned mobile phone at Stella. "What shall we have? Shamrock, lucky horse shoe, rabbit's foot?"

The tinkling of Daphne's phone charms was echoed by another metallic jangling from outside the room.

The door opened and John came in. He stumbled over the black panther. If anyone else had fallen over it, Stella would have apologised from dropping it right inside the doorway but police detectives should be better prepared for potential danger.

"Don't tread on Thirteen; you'll spoil his fur," she snapped.

"Thirteen? It's not Daphne's then. What are you pair of witches up to now and why do you need to involve a poor innocent black cat in whatever it is?" he asked.

"Your sister insisted we have our fortunes told and now she's making me seal it up..." Stella trailed off; why did she constantly try to justify herself to the smug little man? She didn't care what he thought of her.

"You got your fortunes told by mail order?" John asked.

"Don't be silly, we went to see a gypsy at the fair," Stella said.

"Oh yes, far more sensible."

Stella felt her face form a scowl. Being patronised by him was even worse when she agreed with his opinion.

"I think it was sensible," Daphne said. "Gypsy Rosie-Lee has a very good reputation and she gave us this to prove she spoke the truth." Daphne held up the letter.

John snatched it from her and removed it from the purple envelope.

"You can't read it, John! Stella and I agreed we shouldn't know what it said until the year is up so we don't influence the outcome."

"That at least is sensible. Don't worry girls; I won't tell you what it says."

He read it and laughed. "That'll be right."

"What?" they both asked together.

"Thought you were sealing it up because you didn't want to know?" He folded it and handed it back. "Seal it up then and I'll hold on to it. That's fair – not because the pair of you trust me the way you should trust a copper, but because there's no way either of you will be influenced by anything I say."

He had a point. They sealed it with red wax and the shamrock charm and handed it back to him.

Stella sighed. Now how was she supposed to read the stupid thing and make sure none of it came true?

"What's up, Stella?" John asked. "Didn't you want me to korma bahji-ing in to your rice evening?"

"Oh, no. Er, I mean yes," she mumbled.

Belatedly she remembered she'd promised herself she'd be polite to John, mostly for Daphne's sake. She had to get away from him before she got even more flustered and said something she might regret.

"There's some food left and you must be hungry after pounding the beat, shall I put it in the microwave for you?"

Without waiting for an answer, Stella gathered up the foil dishes and headed for the kitchen.

"Keep currying favour like that and I'll give you a lift home," John called to her back.

Great. He really would insist on driving her home instead of allowing her to risk the perils of the properly licensed taxi firm she frequently used. Now she'd have to show gratitude for the lift and later turn on the charm to get him to let her read the gypsy's letter. That promised to be a humiliating experience. Worse was to come, she soon discovered.

Chapter Three

"Stella, talking of lifts... I've got to pick up Gran for Mum and Dad's wedding anniversary party Saturday so I'm not sure I'll be able to collect you."

"No problem, I'll get a bus over." She was working in the morning or she'd have suggested accompanying Daphne. It was a long drive and they'd have been able to have a good chat on the way up and Gran would have kept them entertained on the way back. She loved to tell wildly exaggerated tales of her misspent youth.

"No need, I'll collect you. That's if you can be ready by four?" John said.

"I can, but I don't want to put you out." Didn't want to have to be grateful was more like it.

"You won't be putting me out if you're ready on time. I'll collect you on my way home from work and still have time to change. That means you'll arrive early, but you did offer to help." He somehow managed to imply her offer wasn't genuine.

"That'd be great. I promised your mum I'd do the flowers and anything else she wanted."

So John would have no cause to complain, Stella got ready as soon as she'd eaten her lunch after work. That meant she had a boring hour to sit and wait as she didn't dare start reading a good book or doing anything else that might take her mind off the time. She filled it by thinking of Daphne's parents and the fact they'd been married thirty years almost to the day. What must it feel like to have someone you could rely on at your side for all that time? She hoped that one day she'd know.

At twenty to four, Stella went down to wait outside the flats. Wouldn't do for John to waste valuable seconds getting out the car to buzz her intercom. Once out in the humid air she wished she wasn't quite so early. It wasn't just the temperature, Stella had the uncomfortable feeling she was being watched. She glanced around and was relieved to see only an elderly lady approaching with a small brown dog on a lead. A chihuahua, Stella guessed.

The woman was still too far away for Stella to say 'good afternoon' when she heard loud male voices approaching from the opposite direction. A group of four boys, all with hoods pulled up despite the heat, walked purposefully towards her.

"Here doggy, come for a walk with us," one called.

Stella wasn't particularly reassured to learn she wasn't their target.

The lady stopped as though frozen with fear as the boys jogged up to her.

"Come on, love. Give us your doggy and we'll take him for a proper walk." The tallest boy snatched the lead from the woman's hand and dragged the frightened little dog away.

Where was John when she'd actually be pleased to see him? He couldn't be far away surely.

"Let go!" Stella yelled. "My boyfriend is a policeman and he'll be here any minute."

The boys ran, letting go of the lead, leaving the quivering dog on the opposite side of the road. Stella ran over, picked it up and carried it back to its grateful owner.

"Oh dear, you've got her hairs all over your lovely dress. I'm so sorry."

"It doesn't matter," Stella muttered through gritted teeth as she placed the dog on the pavement and handed over the lead. "Are you all right?"

"I am now Beatrice is safe. Thank you so much my dear."

The lady continued to thank her as the dog jumped up and laddered Stella's stockings.

"Maybe you should go down the police station and report this? Those thugs could have stolen Beatrice," Stella suggested in the hope of getting rid of her new friend.

"Oh, but what about your boyfriend?"

It took Stella a moment to realise what the lady meant. "No policeman boyfriend. Sorry I made him up."

"Oh what a shame."

Stella nodded. "I am going out to a friend's party though and I think I'd better get changed." She went back into her building before John could arrive and make the lady think Stella had been lying to her rather than the boys.

To her relief it was still only ten to four when Stella reached her flat. She threw her dog haired clothes on the floor, pulled on fresh stockings and another dress and dragged a brush through her hair before running back downstairs. John was waiting.

Still out of breath from her dog rescue and quick change, Stella tried to explain what had happened.

"Couldn't you avoid stroking dogs if getting a few hairs on you would make you late?" was his only comment.

Stella bit her lip and stared out the windscreen. Was it only about fifteen minutes ago she was wishing to see him and even less than that she was sounding regretful as she explained she didn't really have a policeman as a boyfriend?

At least the party was fun. She knew many of the guests from previous social occasions with Daphne and her parents. It was lovely when even distant cousins remembered her and treated her like one of the family. The food was fabulous as Daphne had spent hours preparing it. Stella spent much less time on the flowers, but she thought they looked pretty good and, from comments she overheard, it seemed she wasn't alone.

The only thing that marred her fun was John's insistence that he'd drive her home afterwards.

"There's no need, I'll get the late bus back."

"And have to walk the length of the High Street? I don't think so, there might be a kitten to be rescued or something and you'd never make it home."

So he had understood her explanation for holding him up earlier on. Typical John, instead of praising her good deed he'd somehow made the whole thing seem like a problem she'd brought on herself.

As Stella spooned low calorie and flavour-free cereal into her mouth, she flicked through a magazine.

'Trust to fate and things will soon look brighter,' the horoscope promised.

Stella wasn't going to rely on the astrologer's fantasies any more than she was ready to accept the gypsy's promises everything would work out for herself and Daphne. That wasn't going to just happen; life doesn't work that way. Her evening out with Daphne last week must have still been on her mind; otherwise, she'd never have read the horoscopes.

She forced down another mouthful of healthy but bland mush, trying to convince herself it tasted OK.

Daphne would happily drift along leaving everything to chance. It was Stella who knew they couldn't trust fate, so she was the one who'd have to take action. The first step was finding Daphne a new job.

"Endless macaroni cheese and chicken nuggets isn't what I dreamed of in catering college," she'd moaned a few days previously. "I'd love to try something different for a change. Maybe the kind of salad that consists of more than limp lettuce, under-ripe tomato and tough skinned cucumber, or I could do a colourful stir fry."

"Won't the kids eat anything like that?"

"They don't get the choice. I'm always told that's not the sort of thing that's served for school meals."

Stella looked through her magazine for the recipe section and discovered a mouth watering selection of pizza and pasta dishes. Daphne really should get a job somewhere like the new Italian restaurant in the High Street. And yes, she was right that Stella would be more than willing to sample any new recipes Daphne might want to try out. Stella checked her watch; better get a move on if she was going to have time to walk past the premises, and see how close they were to opening, before she had to be at work. Stella dumped her soggy cereal in the bin, inspected her teeth for bits of bran and grabbed her handbag.

Even at eight-thirty in the morning, the air was hot and dry. She'd not walked that way for a few days and was surprised at the progress made on the restaurant. She was especially impressed by the sign giving the name as 'Trio'. Stella knew Daphne would do her utmost to get a job there once Stella reminded her that Gypsy Rosie-Lee said the number three would be lucky. There was an advert and a phone number on the door. Stella sent Daphne a text urging her to 'apply now!' but somehow forgot to mention the advert was for customers rather than staff.

Pleased with herself, Stella grinned at her boss, Mr Clover, as she let herself into the florist's.

"Good morning, Stella. You're nice and early which is very fortunate because this morning's delivery is also early. Would you mind opening up the shop whilst I attend to it? You can take a little longer for lunch to make up the time."

"OK," Stella agreed.

She glanced at her watch. She was a quarter of an hour early. Usually she turned up almost the same time as Mr Clover turned the sign on the door to 'Open'. Stella switched on the till and cleared last week's wilting window display. When she popped out the back to switch on the kettle, she saw that Mr Clover had started preparations for the new display. Stella collected the plastic buckets filled with water and flowers and hauled them into the deep window recess. A couple of labels became detached and she was pleased that she could now distinguish easily between the alstroemeria and gladioli. When she'd started she hadn't even been sure both were flowers. Now she confidently advised customers alstroemerias would last two weeks in a vase, even during the current heat-wave.

She'd planned to simply put the flowers ready for Mr Clover to select and display. Once they were massed together she decided they looked good and so slipped the plastic buckets into the aluminium ones they used for display on the shop floor. She put buckets of red, orange and yellow flowers together in the left corner and white and blue ones on the other side. In the space between, she scattered white and grey pebbles and the stainless steel tools Mr Clover would have used to remove leaves and cut stems. The display looked good she thought. She hoped someone would pass by and see it before Mr Clover had time to decorate the window properly.

"You've done the window!" Mr Clover said on his return.

"I know it's not how you do it, but I thought it looked OK and was better than nothing for now..."

Mr Clover went outside to assess her efforts.

"No, it's not how I'd have done it, but it's tidy and attractive. Well done."

Stella smiled at him again. It was the first time he'd praised her since she'd mastered the till in her first week. There were no fewer customers than usual that morning, so her display hadn't put people off. Actually several people asked for flowers they'd seen in the window.

Stella unpacked the supplies of foam, wire and other flower arrangers' props and checked them off against the delivery note whenever she was without a customer. When she'd done that she made up the next order. As she did so Mr Clover began making wreaths for a funeral. He broke off at eleven to suggest coffee and doughnuts. As he ate his sugary treat he double-checked Stella's paperwork as was his habit, but he gave it only a brief glance.

"Yes, that's fine. Will you ring it through this afternoon?"

Stella nodded. She liked calling the supply company as she always shared a joke or two with the sales girl. Everything was going perfectly fine until John turned up.

"You left this behind the other night," he said, placing her address book on the counter.

"Thanks," she muttered.

He couldn't just let Daphne return it next time she saw her; he had to come round specially to prove she was careless or forgetful or whatever fault he was trying to make a point about. She probably couldn't make things much worse now, so she might as well ask about the letter.

"Isn't Daphne funny, the way she believed all that stuff the gypsy told us?"

"Absolutely hilarious."

By a heroic effort she managed to ignore his sarcasm. "You know that if what the gypsy wrote turns out to be true, she'll never make another move her whole life without checking her horoscope and dealing the cards and..."

"If what the gypsy says is true then she'd have good reason to believe it, wouldn't she? But I think you'll find she's not as gullible as you are cynical."

Ouch. How was it possible that someone she cared nothing about was still able to hurt her?

"Don't worry, I've got the letter perfectly safe," John assured her. "Wouldn't want anyone reading it and trying to manipulate other people's lives. I know how much you hate it when anyone tries to run your life for you."

Double ouch.

Chapter Four

John left Clover's before Stella could come up with a suitable reply, which was probably just as well as he'd have had a long wait.

Once he'd gone, she opened her address book. Had he looked inside to see his own name heavily scored out?

He'd looked. Her book now contained his new number and the pencilled comment, 'I hope you never have a problem, but if you do please call me.' Yeah right, he'd be the first person she'd want to contact in a crisis.

She wasn't sure if she should be more annoyed at him for writing it or herself for the love hearts she'd once drawn around his name and hadn't properly obliterated. He'd probably had a laugh when he'd seen them. Stella could feel the heat of her face but didn't know if it was from anger or embarrassment. She was completely over John, so it wasn't fair he could still have such an impact on her emotions. She'd been fifteen when he'd 'discovered' how manipulative she was. Even if he couldn't see it had been Daphne's plan for Stella and John to marry, so orphaned Stella would have a family, then he could at least credit her with having grown up in the twelve years since.

Stella was surprised and delighted when Daphne called round to say she'd just been offered the position of assistant chef at Trio.

"Rosie-Lee was dead right about three being lucky for me. It's not just the name of the restaurant," she continued when

Stella had nodded noncommittally. "The first time I rang, the person I spoke to didn't know anything about an advertised vacancy."

That didn't surprise Stella as she knew there'd been no advert.

"When I rang again I spoke to Luigi himself. He was obviously busy so I said I'd come in later. When I turned up for my third attempt to apply for the job this evening he interviewed me straight away and said yes!"

That didn't surprise Stella either. What red-blooded Italian restaurant owner would be able to resist her gorgeous and talented blonde friend? Stella pictured him as a charming silver-haired gentlemen with an eye for a pretty girl and the rest of him firmly devoted to a formidable Latin matriarch.

Stella hugged her friend and insisted they go out to celebrate. After an hour and a half of hearing what a wonderful opportunity this was for Daphne and what a wonderful employer it seemed Luigi would be and how she owed it all to Rosie-Lee Stella felt slightly miffed.

"It was me who gave you the number and nagged you to call, remember."

"Of course I remember. I was really surprised at you for wanting me to go along with what Rosie-Lee aid. Why did you?"

"Because I thought it would be a good job for you. You've shown more enthusiasm for this Trio in the couple of hours since you got the job than in all the time you worked at the school."

"Well it is a great opportunity and Luigi, my boss, is lovely and sounds really supportive. You are pleased for me, aren't you?"

"I am. Just as pleased as I was the last eighteen times you asked me that!"

"Oh. Have I been going on?"

"Yes, but it's OK, because I think you're right and I'M VERY PLEASED FOR YOU!'

As Stella had anticipated, Daphne regularly popped in to Stella's flat to chat during her breaks from work in the early evening before the restaurant became too busy for her to be spared. Stella always hoped she'd hear the building's intercom buzzer, rather than Daphne's voice announcing her arrival. Although Daphne was welcome anytime, she was doubly so when clutching so much food she couldn't fish out Stella's spare key to let herself in through the outer door on street level. Sometimes it was samples of new items the restaurant was trying out, occasionally it was food left over from the previous evening.

Stella enjoyed having her friend visit regularly and not just because of the tasty treats. It was good to see her feeling so positive. Stella felt slightly smug over her part in encouraging Daphne to change jobs to one which far better suited her talents and personality.

"The fortune teller was right, Stella. I'm really happy there," Daphne said while Stella made her a cup of tea to go with the tiny almond cookies brought from Trio.

"One of the things that put me off working in a proper restaurant was the unsocial hours. But actually that's proving to be an advantage. Late finishes and late starts suit me and I get time off in the afternoon when the shops are quieter. Getting there is much easier too and not just because it's closer. Of course the actual job is much better. Really lovely food for people who actually enjoy it and...."

"OK, I believe it's a great job! You forget it was me who suggested it."

"Only after the fortune teller put the idea in your head. Talking of which, Luigi is tall, dark and handsome. And his accent." Daphne sighed. "It has the same effect on me as drinking Amaretto."

Stella stopped nibbling and leant forward. "Luigi?" she asked. Not a silver-haired charming old gentleman then. She should have guessed it was more than balsamic dressing putting a sparkle into Daphne's eyes.

"My new boss. That's what the gypsy meant about our lives being entwined. Come in and meet him, Stella."

Tempting idea. This Luigi sounded a little too good to be true but if he was for real, he'd be perfect for Daffs. She'd have to check him out without giving away her intentions. For that she'd better not seem too eager.

"That's what I meant by a self-fulfilling prophesy. You never introduced me to your last boss, but you're introducing me to this one because of what the gypsy said." In her agitation, Stella slopped tea onto the turquoise throw she'd draped over her old sofa to hide red wine stains. She dashed to the kitchen and grabbed a handful of kitchen roll and dabbed at the damp spot.

Daphne helped by pulling the material flat and checking Thirteen's furry head for splashes.

"Maybe you were right about him being lucky. He's escaped from a Tetley shower."

"He's not lucky. He's just a cat and I'm not quite as clumsy as you seem to think."

Daphne pointed to the damp spot on Stella's knee. "I didn't introduce you to my last boss because he was a disgusting sleaze bag with bad breath and an unnatural interest in mathematical formula. I'm not trying to introduce you to my new one because of what she said, but because she's right. He's gorgeous."

"So why not chat him up yourself? It's obvious you're interested."

"I can't; it's not my destiny. Besides my stars say I shouldn't be looking for love this month, but that it'll find me when I least expect it. You just don't want to meet him because you're worried you'll fall for him and that would make the gypsy right."

Stella nibbled another of the delicious biscuits. "These are fab."

"Luigi made them."

"All right, all right. I'll meet him. He probably won't fancy me anyway." And maybe having a bit of competition would encourage Daphne to take an interest in him herself. Not that Stella would in any way match-make; the girls had long since promised each other not to make that mistake again.

"Come round tomorrow at five-thirty," Daphne suggested. "It's quiet then and I'll just be prepping veg and be able to talk to you and introduce him. I know you'll like him; it's impossible not to."

The following day Stella persuaded Mr Clover to allow her to finish slightly early. Because she'd arrived early three mornings that week and helped open up the shop, he was happy to agree. She rushed home to change.

She'd had the sense to leave the clothes she wanted to wear on the bed, so only had to drag them on, smooth her hair and top up her lippy and mascara. As Stella opened the street door at the bottom of the stairway, she knocked into a man wearing a donkey jacket. She'd seen him before, hanging about outside her building. Just like last time, he didn't look at her or speak when she apologised for startling him. She hoped his hanging about didn't mean he was about to move into the flat below her. Although it would be nice to have someone living there instead of a load of packing cases, she'd rather it wasn't him; he gave her the creeps. Stella shrugged and crossed the street towards Trio.

She got two surprises when she arrived. The first was seeing Daphne in her chef's whites, clogs and massive floppy hat. She looked both professional and cute. Alberto was the second surprise. He was the six foot five, twenty stone head chef. Hearing Daphne talk about Trio she'd formed the opinion that it was just Luigi she worked with in the kitchen. Instead there was Alberto running the kitchen, a boy washing up and fetching and carrying, another responsible for preparing vegetables and salads and assembling bread and olives, and waiters popping in to check on the ingredients of each dish so they could properly advise customers. It wasn't long however before the owner himself appeared in the gleaming white and steel kitchen.

Daphne was right; Luigi was tall, dark and very attractive. He fussed around Stella, pouring her a glass of cool Pinot Grigio and despatching the boy porter to bring a chair so she could sit in a corner of the kitchen, out the way, but close enough to Daphne to chat. Horrified to learn Stella hadn't eaten, Luigi directed Daphne to show off her skill and make a plate of bruschetta.

Luigi produced a foot high pepper grinder and seasoned the food with a flourish before encouraging Stella to eat. She smiled at him, trying not to flutter her lashes too obviously. A man who didn't like to see a woman go hungry was Stella's idea of a catch, especially when his face and voice were as appealing as the food. She watched his back view appreciatively as he left the kitchen. Perhaps Daphne was right about it being not being her destiny to date her boss and that the stars favoured a match between him and Stella. She sighed; sometimes a girl just had to accept her fate.

"Wow, this is delicious, Daffs..." she said between mouthfuls of the snack and sips of a second glass of wine. "And your Luigi is quite tasty too."

"Told you!"

"You didn't tell him to be nice to me because it's his destiny, did you?"

"No! And you needn't let his charm go to your head; he's nearly as nice to John when he comes in to visit me."

Stella tried to heed her friend's advice, but it was difficult when Luigi kissed her hand in farewell and begged her to return soon. It didn't take Stella long to decide she was being unfair to Daphne in encouraging her to give up so many of her breaks to visit the flat and that it was only fair for Stella to visit her at Trio occasionally.

If anything, Luigi was even more charming on Stella's second visit. All his most extravagant compliments were made when Daphne was close enough to hear, which was a good job. Stella wouldn't have been able to keep a straight face when reporting her complexion was 'smoother and creamier than mascarpone, that the sight of her warmed Luigi 'more than the pizza ovens' and her eyes 'sparkled brighter than crystal glasses gleaming in candlelight'.

Chapter Five

Daphne rang Stella at work the following morning. "Will you come round to see me at Trio again tonight? I'm going to make sun-dried tomato and basil soup. You could have some for your tea."

"What do you want?"

"Stella! I don't want any... Oh, all right, but it's Luigi, not me. I'm sure he wants to ask you out. He dropped lots of hints asking if we both had boyfriends and what we liked to do in our spare time."

"He asked about both of us?"

"Yes. I tell you, he's really keen on you."

If Stella believed in fate she'd have been hard pushed to say whether it was conspiring for or against her. It was Daphne's life Stella wanted to sort out, but Luigi was very attractive. Stella wasn't sure she'd be able to turn him down if he asked, especially as Daphne seemed so sure he wasn't the man for her. Just as Stella was about to reply, Mr Clover came into the shop to announce a big delivery had arrived.

"Gotta go, Daffs." Stella dropped her phone into her bag and turned her attention back to work.

As well as the usual flowers, the driver suggested Mr Clover buy potted herbs.

"Someone over ordered, so we're selling them cheap."

"They do look nice," Stella said. "And there's nowhere else in town that sells pot plants." If she was manager here instead of a lowly assistant with no prospects she'd be looking for opportunities to increase business.

"You can even take them on sale or return," the driver added, finally persuading Mr Clover.

Stella arranged a few pots on the counter. Every time she reached over to give a customer their wrapped flowers or take payment, her hand brushed against the basil, releasing its appetising aroma. Stella couldn't help thinking of Daphne's encouragement to pop into the restaurant that evening. She arrived at Trio wanting soup before Daphne had finished chopping the tomatoes.

As Daphne had hinted, Luigi did appear very interested in her. He had his priorities right too. He made sure her stomach was settled with soup and focaccia bread, scented with fresh thyme, before trying to unsettle her heart with smooth words delivered in his even smoother Italian accent. She tried not to giggle when he compared her to balsamic vinegar and himself to lettuce awakened by her sweetness. She glanced over at her friend so see if she showed signs of jealousy. Daphne just grinned and gave her a thumbs up behind Luigi's back. Stella ensured she didn't make eye contact with Daphne when he described himself as a marble edifice whose strength was eroded by Stella in the guise of a Venetian canal. Stella reluctantly left the kitchen when orders began flooding in. Luigi opened the door for her and whispered an invitation to go out with him. She had no hesitation in accepting. Daphne clearly didn't want him and he was too much man to go to waste on anyone other than one of them.

Stella took a day off work to prepare herself and her flat for her first date with Luigi. She hoovered the carpet and shaved her legs, shoved all her junk under the bed and selected her nicest underwear. Taking advantage of the lack of neighbours below her flat she turned up her music and sang along as she worked.

By the time the buzzer on her cooker sounded to tell her it was time to stop making the bed and start making up her face, the flat looked every bit as good as it had the day she moved in. Better, because since then she'd added colourful cushions, paintings of tropical beaches and lots of scented candles. Everything went well: she hadn't chipped a nail while scrubbing her kitchen floor, she didn't poke herself in the eye with a mascara brush and the zip on her dress didn't break. When she looked in the mirror at the finished result she wondered why she'd been single for so long. Fortunately she didn't have enough time to wonder that she came up with a confidence undermining answer.

Luigi buzzed her intercom exactly on time. He quickly climbed the stairs, gave a slight bow when he saw her waiting in the open doorway and offered her a bunch of white roses.

"Thank you, they're lovely. Come in a moment while I put them in water."

He smiled, but waited in the hallway while she attended to the flowers.

Luigi took her to a restaurant which specialised in seafood. Although she was glad her date and best friend hadn't spent hours discussing her, she couldn't help wishing he'd asked for advice over the best place to take her. Maybe after seeing her tuck in at Trio, he'd assumed, almost correctly, she would eat anything. Fortunately the 'Oyster Over Easy' offered a vegetarian option and Stella wasn't forced to chew her way through a lump of gristle that, until recently, carried its own home around wherever it went. The expression on Luigi's face after he asked where she worked suggested he too wished he'd done some research and brought her a gift of chocolates instead of flowers.

Conversation flowed more easily when they talked about Daphne. Luigi laughed when Stella described some of the scrapes Daphne's faith in the stars had led them to.

"She truly believes these things?" Luigi asked.

"Gosh, yes. For a while her parents' house was almost entirely green because Daphne's stars said that colour would bring luck. We painted her bedroom and dyed our underwear. We didn't make a good job of either and there was paint and dye spread everywhere. The more we tried to clean it up the further we spread it."

Luigi gestured extravagantly, presumably indicating his horror. "Her mother, she was angry?"

"No, luckily Daffs' mum isn't like that and anyway, her brother saw it first and helped with the clearing up."

"Ah yes. John is a very practical man."

"I suppose. Very annoying though."

Luigi shrugged. "And Daphne, she never painted your house?"

"No. I lived with different foster families, so mostly we went to hers."

"Foster? That is you have no family? This is a terrible thing."

"No it's OK. I've never known any different and I've got Daffs. Her and her parents have been like family to me since we started school."

"And John? He is your big brother and so that is why he annoys you?"

Stella nodded. That was so much easier than explaining John was nothing like a brother to her and that there were so many different ways he annoyed her.

The waiter appeared to ask if they'd like to see the dessert menu. Luigi's, "but of course," soon made Stella forget about past irritations and concentrate instead on forthcoming pleasure.

"I'm going for the mango crème brûlée. Creamy and toffee-ey and almost one of my five a day."

"You eat five desserts a day?" Luigi asked.

She'd started explaining the government's healthy eating advice before she saw he was teasing her.

When the waiter offered coffee Luigi further went up in Stella's estimation by saying, "Please, and my friend will require plenty of cream and chocolates with hers."

After the meal, which he insisted on paying for, Luigi took her to watch a romantic film. He bought tickets for the back row and fussed around ensuring she was comfortable. Stella smirked at the heroine's token attempts at resisting the all action hero. Afterwards Luigi took her home and said goodbye without acting out any of the scenes from the film. He did however ask her to come out with him again the following week.

Unusually Daphne didn't interrogate her over every detail of the evening.

"It would seem odd knowing all the details when I work with him."

Mr Clover could probably have managed without any details at all but Stella had to talk to someone so she found herself mentioning Luigi, the food they'd eaten and the film they'd watched throughout the next few days.

"I am glad you are happy, Stella. Recently you have seemed a little... discontent."

"Just bored, I suppose. Sometimes there's not much to do here, is there?"

"No, no there isn't."

Stella and Luigi's second date was less awkward, but no more amorous. By the third, she realised he was determined to be a perfect gentleman and decided he was romantic in his own, subtle way.

Luigi took her boating on the lake and sang to her like a gondolier. He could have seemed comical, singing in Italian what sounded like spring love songs on a grey lake on a grey afternoon in an English autumn; somehow he didn't. Even when he recited poetry to her, Luigi didn't seem ridiculous. He flirted extravagantly, smiled seductively and gazed into her eyes. It wasn't only the rocking motion of the boat making her conscious her feet weren't firmly on the ground. She felt like the romantic heroine in some arty film.

Stella fell into Luigi's arms as he helped her out of the small boat. He held her close and grinned as though sure she hadn't stumbled accidentally. Maybe he was right.

"Sorry, it's past lunchtime and I'm weak with hunger," she joked to hide her embarrassment.

"Then we shall eat."

He'd prepared a hamper containing a flask of piping hot minestrone soup, fresh herb rolls, delicate wafers of ham and a selection of fresh fruit.

Whenever Trio was closed and Stella wasn't at the florist's, Luigi took her out. He sent her roses, Italian chocolate truffles and poetic notes. The romance was all on the surface though, at the end of each evening he kissed her politely and went home. It seemed that he knew the way to her heart but didn't want to travel there, or to any other part of her body. That was kind of weird, but so was her own behaviour. With another man she'd have been making none too subtle hints that they could have even more fun staying in than by going out, but with Luigi it didn't seem quite right.

"Luigi," she asked as he walked her home one moonlit night, "You really do like me, don't you?"

"Of course. Don't we have fun together, go nice places, laugh, dance?"

"Yes, but I meant do you like me as a girlfriend?"

Luigi took her hand and turned to face her. "I am very fond of you, Stella. It's just that I think we shouldn't rush into anything. You have just come out of a relationship, I understand?"

Stella nodded. She'd told him she'd split up with her last boyfriend a couple of months before meeting Luigi. She hadn't been exactly heartbroken, but she didn't want Luigi to get the impression she was a tart. If she wanted someone to give her unwanted relationship advice she could always ask John.

"There was recently someone I cared for very much, but she doesn't feel the same way," Luigi said.

"Oh, I see." She squeezed his hand. "I know how that feels." It wasn't Kevin she was referring to, but Luigi didn't need to know that.

So she'd been right, he didn't really fancy her. To be honest, although she found him incredibly charming and gorgeous to look at she didn't really fancy him either. It was almost like having a crush on a pop star; fun to fantasise about but not a relationship you'd expect to work in real life. At least she told herself it was something like that and not just sour grapes that he wasn't physically attracted to her.

Luigi was very nice, fun to be with and generous, so if he wanted to keep taking her out she was happy to help him get over the girl who'd apparently broken his heart.

Luigi often took her for drives in the country or to restaurants and concerts, then he took her home; and left her there alone. She wasn't sure if that would ever change. She wasn't even sure if she wanted it to.

Stella enjoyed talking to Luigi about their very different upbringings. Luigi made her laugh with stories about his younger siblings and older members of his extended family. She agreed they sounded wonderful and that he must miss them all terribly. He told her about the beautiful scenery, artwork and buildings in his native Florence. Stella said how much she'd like to go there.

"Stella, you would adore it as I do. Imagine strolling through the Boboli Gardens past the statues and fountains or visiting our *Duomo*, the *Basilica di Santa Maria del Fiore*."

She understood a garden with fountains and thought it sounded nice, but had no idea what the rest meant. Presumably it was some pretty tourist spot, maybe a nice view so she smiled and nodded.

"We could even walk along the beautiful Ponte Vecchio and you could buy lovely things in the shops."

Buying souvenirs! Now he was talking her language. "Ponte, that means bridge, doesn't it?"

"Yes, but not just any bridge. It is the most beautiful bridge in all of Italy. The whole world."

"Not that you're biased at all."

"No. It is the truth. *Fiorentini* know that their city is the most beautiful, their treasures the most precious. But everyone feels like that about their home."

Stella didn't. She was quite prepared to believe that the gardens, buildings and bridges that Luigi loved were more beautiful that the High Street and park of her home town.

"Oh, there's a huge picture of a pretty bridge in Trio, is that the Ponte Vecchio?"

Luigi laughed.

"Sorry, did I say it wrong?"

"No. That picture is of the Bridge of Sighs. Pretty as you say, but not beautiful like the bridges of Florence. It is more famous though, amongst those who think Venice is the place for romance."

"Ah, but they'd be wrong though, because Florence is much more beautiful and far more romantic?" she said to try to make up for having previously believed that Venice was indeed the place for romance.

"You are right, but I think you tease me?"

Stella gave what she hoped was an innocently charming smile.

"In England you do not love the place where you were born?"

"I moved about quite a lot after I was taken into care and I was still little, maybe that makes a difference."

"Of course. I'm sorry I should not have said that."

"It's all right, Luigi really."

"And Daphne, she is your sister. Spiritual sister?"

"Oh yes, she's spiritual all right." Stella grinned. She wasn't sure if he'd meant that as a pun, but his answering smile showed that he got the joke even if he hadn't intended it.

Luigi was interested to hear about her childhood with her foster parents and the escapades she and Daphne got up to.

"My foster mum pretended not to know I climbed out my bedroom window and went out with Daphne to the fair. It wasn't until years later she admitted she knew and used to ask Daphne's brother to keep an eye on us."

Luigi was sorry Stella had no family and insisted she came in to the restaurant early on Sunday lunchtimes to share the staff meal.

"My staff, they are like my English family," he told her.

"Great, because Daphne is like family to me," Stella said.

When Stella arrived for the first lunch, she was surprised to see most of the restaurant tables stacked at the side of the dining area. Everyone was crowded together round a long table down the centre, like a family meal in a TV advert for pasta sauce.

"All the family together," Luigi said, just as Stella noticed John was one of the guests.

Luigi looked so pleased with himself, Stella couldn't possibly admit she hadn't meant the whole family thing so literally.

"I propose the toast to Stella *bellissima*," Luigi said. He poured the contents of a frosted glass jug into cocktail glasses. "This my special cocktail 'Stella Sparkler'. It is sweet, sparkling, tempting and just a little bit naughty."

Stella blushed and Daphne giggled.

John refused to try the drink because he was on duty.

"John, you are right not to taste if you cannot quench your thirst. Just a sip of Stella will never ever be enough."

Poor John, he didn't seem to be enjoying his glass of coke as much as she was enjoying her cocktail. She took another sip. It was getting sweeter by the minute.

Chapter Six

Neither Daphne nor Luigi had taken many evenings off work since he'd opened Trio. Stella was concerned that Daphne's free evenings were spent with her. It wasn't that she wasn't pleased to spend time with her friend; she was. She just wished Daphne had a boyfriend to spend her time with. Daphne claimed she was quite happy as she was and in any case she didn't have time for dates in the evening or the chance to meet anyone.

"Go out in the day then, like Luigi and I do. What about someone at work?"

"Alberto is married."

"What about the waiters, some of them are cute or that guy in charge of the wine, he's gorgeous."

"Is he?"

"Daphne, what's wrong with you?"

"Nothing. Why?"

"You're looking better than ever and surrounded by attractive men but you don't notice them and you're obviously not sending out the right signals..."

"Don't worry about me, Stells please. Just accept there might not be a man on the scene for a while. Anyway, how are you and Luigi getting on? You've hardly told me anything."

That was because she'd received no encouragement to do so. She hoped Daphne's interest in her love life might spark some enthusiasm for romance herself and resolved to paint as rosy a picture as possible.

Luigi's apparent desire to spend his free evenings with Stella was a lot less troubling. She was flattered when he chose to do so just to take her dancing. From the moment Luigi arrived, looking and smelling wonderful and clutching a slender bouquet of exotic blue flowers, Stella knew the evening would be romantic and wanted to remember every detail to share with Daphne.

"The colour reminds me of your eyes, although no flower could be as beautiful," Luigi murmured as he presented the flowers.

He kissed her cheek and admired her dress before escorting her down the stairs from her flat and opening his car door for her.

They enjoyed a candlelit supper and shared a bottle of wine. Actually, because Luigi was driving, Stella enjoyed more than her fair share. Afterwards he took her to a classy nightclub where, instead of having to queue in the cold evening air, Luigi had a brief word with the doorman who ushered them straight in. Was there no one who didn't instantly surrender to his charm?

Stella could feel the slow thud of his heart and the warmth of his body as she danced in Luigi's arms.

"*I vostri capelli sono scuri e dolcemente profumata come una notte di primavera*," Luigi whispered.

"That sounds very romantic. What does it mean?"

"Your hair is as dark and softly fragrant as a spring night." Luigi ran his fingers through her loose hair as he spoke.

"Aaaw, that's nice." Stella couldn't help wondering if those words would have sounded just as good whispered by any handsome man whose accent happened to be as sexy as Luigi's. "I'm glad I washed it after work now." She was.

Luigi wasn't just any handsome Italian man - he was the only one holding her in his arms and whispering in her ear. She snuggled a little closer to his trim body.

If she and Luigi were acting in a film, they'd need soft lighting and subtitles. Stella decided this was the point where the credits should roll and Daphne would simply have to imagine the rest of the details.

"Would you like another drink?" Luigi asked when the song finished.

"Nothing alcoholic this time, I have to get up for work tomorrow."

"Coffee?" Luigi said.

"I'm not sure they serve it here."

"No, I don't think they do. I have a Gaggia in my apartment."

"A what?"

"A coffee machine, Stella. I could take you to my apartment and brew something up." He gave a wicked smile.

This time no subtitles were needed; he was offering more than a hot drink.

Luigi's home could have been arranged especially for a double page spread in a fashion magazine entitled 'Italian restaurant owner's bachelor pad'. It was all white walls, expensive chrome gadgets and stylish black furniture. Black rugs were scattered across the polished wood floor. Scattered with the aid of a protractor and foot rule, she wouldn't mind betting. The lighting was soft and the air pleasantly scented.

Black framed monochrome prints of old buildings and landscapes only slightly relieved the starkness of the walls. One was of the leaning tower of Pisa, another showed a bridge and she wondered if that was the Ponte Vecchio.

The spacious living room was dominated by a huge couch in black leather, heaped with luxurious silk, fur and suede cushions all in shades of grey. Such stylish surroundings were very Luigi. She imagined the bed would be huge and low, with black satin sheets and yet more neatly arranged, grey cushions.

Stella was glad she was wearing yellow; if she'd opted for her little black dress she might have worried he'd only invited her back because she matched the decor.

"Would you like to put on some music, Stella?" he asked.

She watched him walk through a large archway into a gleaming white kitchen, decorated with strings of garlic and tall bottles of herb flavoured oils. The flat, like Luigi himself, seemed slightly unreal. It was far too neat and tidy for a normal man. Even here she wasn't sure she was any closer to knowing him. Luigi placed two delicate cups on his coffee machine, then turned to smile at her as though aware he was being observed.

Eventually she discovered his chrome stereo housed in a discrete black cabinet in the corner of his living room. By the time she'd selected something which looked from the cover as though it might be romantic and set the volume to low, Luigi was sprawled on the couch.

"Come, sit with me," he said, holding a hand towards her.

"Be right there."

Stella slipped into the bathroom, where she checked her teeth were free from food, gargled with breath freshener and brightened her make-up. When she returned, Luigi was asleep. She watched him for a moment, even in sleep he was beautiful. She gently brushed his hair of his cheek and bent to kiss him. He didn't stir. She sat beside him until she heard the coffee machine hiss. After switching that off she decided it had sounded better than the CD which she guessed was opera. She didn't want Luigi thinking she was an opera fan. If he did, he'd probably take her to see one, without bothering to check she wanted to go, and it might be Stella's turn to fall asleep. She turned off the stereo and returned the CD to the shelf.

Luigi awoke. "Stella, I am so sorry. What must you think?"

"That you're tired?"

"Yes that is true. We've been so busy at work that it's always two in the morning or later when I get to sleep."

"Then you'd better go to bed now."

"Yes, but I will drive you home first."

"There's no need."

"You prefer to walk?"

Although it would only take her ten minutes, that hadn't been what she'd had in mind, but it seemed to be her only option. "Thanks for a lovely evening and for my flowers. Goodnight." She kissed his cheek and let herself out.

It was only as she was crossing the road to her flat she realised she could have curled up beside him on his sofa as he slept. If she'd done so, his reaction on waking might have been very different.

The next morning, Stella sent Daphne a text saying she wanted to talk to her as soon as she was free, then took the flowers Luigi gave her into work. Mr Clover had told her about the language of flowers, explaining a red rose meant true love, a carnation symbolised rejection and that his own name represented diligence. Maybe there was a hidden meaning behind the flowers she'd been given. She'd ask him after they'd finished setting up the Hallowe'en display.

Stella had the idea for stocking spooky blooms after a customer asked for black flowers for a dinner party at the end of October. Mr Clover had looked a little less tired than usual when he said it was a good suggestion and allowed her to order extra stock. The window soon boasted a selection of mini pumpkins and blood red and eerily black flowers. These were supported by fiendishly spiky foliage and decorative twigs bound together to represent witches brooms.

"What are these, Mr Clover?" Stella said, showing him the flowers Luigi had given her. "They look like orchids, but I've only ever seen white or pink ones."

"Gosh, those are a very vivid blue. I'm not surprised you were confused. They are Singapore orchids, so you were correct. Their natural colour is white."

"Oh, so these aren't real. I put them in water, how daft am I?"

Mr Clover felt a blossom between his thumb and forefinger. "They are real. They will have been dyed. The flowers do come in a range of pink shades, but usually white are grown so that they can be dyed to any colour."

"Are the pink ones we sell natural?"

"Yes. I prefer flowers to be in natural colours."

She didn't ask him what the orchids might mean in the language of flowers; if the flowers had been altered, maybe the meaning had too.

"Your friend Luigi gave them to you?"

"Yes," Stella said.

"Perhaps he chose them to match your eyes?"

Stella nodded.

"He seems a nice man and very fond of you."

Good grief, even reserved Mr Clover had fallen for the irresistible Luigi charm.

"I suppose to match my eyes was a good reason to choose them. It doesn't matter they aren't quite real."

Actually, that made them all the more appropriate as her relationship with Luigi didn't feel completely real either.

John was one of the first customers. He was real all right; a real pain in the neck. He selected a mixed bunch of flowers in palest pink.

"Would you wrap them for me, please, Stella?"

"Of course, would you like a card?"

She didn't see what he wrote inside, but she noticed the tiny envelope was addressed to 'Lucy'.

"Daphne will be relieved," she told Mr Clover once John had left.

"Your friend worries about her brother?"

"Too right she does. She'll be glad John's got a girlfriend now and won't spend so much time moping around their flat. I'm pleased too, of course. John is a decent bloke for the right woman. Obviously that woman is the complete opposite to me. He can be so annoying..."

She trailed off when she saw Mr Clover was looking rather surprised. She couldn't blame him, they didn't usually talk about anything more personal than a polite enquiry into each other's health at the start of each week. At least they hadn't; Mr Clover seemed to know a bit about Luigi and Daphne, so maybe she chattered more now than when she'd first started working for him.

"See what I mean. He's annoyed me again now, by making me spill my guts out to you."

She didn't want Mr Clover to think her personal life was in danger of taking up all her work time so quickly offered to help prepare some of the flowers that had been delivered that morning.

Luigi visited the shop mid-afternoon, just as Stella was trimming long-stemmed white roses. He apologised again for falling asleep. Stella nodded, but kept her attention on her work. She hadn't quite worked out whether she was disappointed or relieved that she and Luigi were still not on more intimate terms than they were after their first date so wasn't sure how she should react.

She'd snapped off the surplus leaves, removed the thorns and re-cut the ends of three stems before Luigi spoke again.

"What film would you like to see on Saturday morning?"

"Sorry, I can't." Stella looked up and smiled to show she wasn't just saying no because she was annoyed he'd fallen asleep.

"We could see something amusing. You'd like that."

Stella was too rough with the tiny pliers she was using and instead of the thorn snapping cleanly away, it was ripped off leaving a tear in the stem.

"I will make rosewater bonbons for us to eat," Luigi said, reverting to his Italian accent.

Didn't it ever occur to the man she might have other plans? Stella studied the damaged stem until she felt able to answer calmly.

"I'll be able to eat the sweets, just not on Saturday morning. I'm going shopping with Daphne. Daffs and I don't get together as often as we'd like."

"Of course you must see your lovely friend."

"She is lovely, but I'm not sure you should tell your girlfriend that. Some girls would get jealous. Actually, I do sometimes wonder why you asked me out and not her," Stella teased. She picked up another rose and stripped off the lower leaves.

"Yes, you are very much alike. To look at, both beautiful but different, inside just the same. Except you say yes, but Daphne, she is not interested in me that way," Luigi said.

That wasn't exactly the answer Stella had hoped for, but maybe Luigi was teasing her too? She never could tell when he was being serious.

"You will buy shoes?" he asked.

This time she knew he was teasing.

"Of course. We're girls. It's our job!"

"And then you will show me them and I will say they are nice, but really they look just like the ones from yesterday."

"Nooo, they'll have a completely different heel, or a diamante trim or..."

"And they'll be very nice. I understand."

After he'd gone she picked up the rose she'd damaged. It couldn't be sold as it was because the tear in the stem meant it wouldn't last very long. It seemed a shame to waste what was otherwise a perfect creamy white bud though. She snipped through the stem just above where the thorn had been and put the flower in water. Mr Clover might be able to use it to make a buttonhole.

When the girls went shopping they didn't actually buy any shoes. Instead they tried on clothes and discussed Luigi.

"Daffs, does he ever mention me?"

"Only all the flippin' time!"

"What does he say?"

"All that bella Stella stuff and how shiny your hair feels."

"Huh!"

"He does."

"He might say it but let me tell you, he's only ever touched my hair once and the rest of me not at all. He told me once about someone he cared for but who didn't feel the same way. I can't remember how he phrased it."

"What's it matter how he said it? He's with you now and over her."

"I'm not sure about that. He doesn't seem to fancy me at all and well, I was wondering if he might be gay?"

Daphne shrieked with laughter. It seemed like minutes before she stopped laughing and could speak. "Luigi?" was all she managed before her mascara streaked face was taken over by giggles. "No, Stella. Luigi most certainly is not gay."

"Well, what's the matter with him then? There was me imagining a passionate Latin lover and he's better behaved than all the supposedly boring British blokes. Or is it me?"

"Don't be daft. Oh, Stells, are things really going badly?"

"I suppose not, I'm probably just being silly."

"Yeah. Hey look at this bag, isn't it great?"

Stella took it from the rail and put it over her shoulder.

"Fabulous. I've got quite a few bags already though, maybe I should save my money for clothes."

"OK then. Next shop."

The next store they visited was a tiny boutique with a display of clothes all in shades of grey.

"This reminds me of Luigi's flat, you should see it," Stella said.

"Don't you like it?" Daphne asked.

"Yeah, it's amazing. Doesn't seem like the home of a real person though; it's just too stylish."

"Luigi is stylish. I wouldn't expect him to live anywhere that wasn't."

"True, I just felt like I didn't really belong."

"You do! Now come on, let's get you something to overshadow Luigi's interior decorating."

In one shop the assistant handed Stella a top to add to the two items she was already carrying.

"Sorry, you have to take three things in. It's company policy," the girl said as Stella grimaced at the puce crocheted number.

For a laugh, she pulled on the baggy top and modelled it over the turquoise skirt she was thinking of buying.

"Do you think Luigi would fancy me in this?" she asked Daphne.

"I reckon he'd fancy you in anything, he seems pretty keen."

Luigi might seem keen, Stella thought as she removed the hideous top, but he hadn't ever seen any of her pretty lace underwear. Once back in her own clothes, Stella said, "I'm still not sure Luigi's as keen as you think. He's really sweet to me and says the most romantic things and I think he's really serious, then he'll mention you and somehow I think bella Stella comes second to the unobtainable Daphne."

"Don't be silly, he's always raving about you at work. Maybe he just says nice things about me to make you jealous?" Daphne said.

"I hadn't thought of that. Fancy me falling for it."

"You've always said one of us is gullible."

Chapter Seven

It seemed to Stella as though she hadn't seen Daphne for weeks.

"Daphne works very hard. I have time off and leave her to work," Luigi said.

"You're a slave driver," Stella told him.

"But Daphne, she does not mind. She likes to cook and likes that you and I are happy."

That was all true. Daphne would be nearly as pleased Stella was having fun as she would be to go out on dates herself. Good job too, as Daphne hadn't gone out on a date since before she'd started her new job. Partly it was, as she'd said, because she was very busy, but there was more to it than that. The normally happy-go-lucky Daphne had suddenly become very picky, as though she'd set her heart on one particular man and no one else could measure up to Mr Perfect. Stella hoped that if her guess was right, the one particular man, whoever he was, would soon see sense and ask her out.

As a distraction from the disappointment of no girly nights with Daphne, Stella was regularly invited out by Luigi. They did eventually see the film Luigi wanted to take her to. It was a bit arty for her, but she'd have happily watched the test card for two hours provided she'd had a supply of Luigi's home-made rose-water bonbons.

Stella and Luigi went to an art gallery full of Italian paintings. Stella stifled a giggle when Luigi told her the names of the artists. They all sounded like types of coffee.

She picked up a brochure for Daphne; she could tell the difference between an impressionist and modern art and might like to visit the gallery sometime. Maybe her mystery man might take her, if there really was a mystery man.

"I understand it is your birthday soon; do you have any plans for your celebration?" Luigi said.

She'd hoped Daphne would be able to take the evening off work and they'd go to a firework display as they usually did. As that wasn't possible, she was going to miss the traditional November ooohing and aaahing with Daphne.

"Not yet."

"I will think of something."

She guessed he'd take her to a firework display if she asked, but with Luigi she wouldn't be able to eat the rubbishy hot-dogs she and Daphne would have shared. He'd probably prepare a sophisticated warm salad to eat in his immaculate flat before they left. Requesting junk food afterwards would seem rude.

"Would you like to attend a firework display? Daphne said that you enjoy them and I understand the one at Middleton Park is considered excellent."

Bless him, he was trying to please her and this time he'd bothered to check she didn't have other plans. She would just have to suffer a sophisticated supper. Somehow she knew it wouldn't be too difficult.

"That would be lovely. Thank you."

As she'd guessed, Luigi did prepare them a meal in his flat. It wasn't a salad, but it was very, very tasty.

"What's that stuff that looks like grated cheese?" she asked, trying not to rush the wonderful pasta. "It's fab."

"White truffle."

"Really? You do mean those ugly wrinkly things that Daphne showed me and said are more expensive than caviar?"

"Precisely."

"They taste better than they look," she admitted. "A lot better."

"I am glad you approve."

Was he laughing at her? She could never tell what he was thinking.

"I hope you will like how this looks," Luigi said. He removed her empty plate and placed a tiny gift wrapped parcel in its place.

She stared at what looked like a ring box.

"Happy birthday, Stella."

"Oh, yes. Thank you."

She slowly removed the shimmering bow and glossy paper. Inside was a felt covered box in the same colour as used by the jewellery shop two doors down from Clover's. Stella shoved her hands under the table and clenched her fists tight to stop them shaking.

After a moment, she was calm enough to open the box. Candlelight caught the jewels giving the impression Luigi had captured a rainbow. She blinked and saw a dozen or more tiny, clear, jewels attached to a web of fine gold chain in an asymmetrical starburst.

"It's a firework!"

"It seemed appropriate."

"It's lovely. Oh thank you. It's so beautiful."

With care, she removed the jewel from its box and saw the gold chain was attached to a delicate pin so it could be worn as a brooch. Could crystals sparkle so brightly? Stella wouldn't dare look in the jeweller's window in case she discovered they were anything else.

"Thank you. I love it."

He had such a lovely smile.

"You are welcome. I was going to ask if you would like dessert."

"But you're not going to?"

"It is tiramisu, so the question is unnecessary."

She might not understand him, but he had her sussed. There was barely time for coffee before they had to leave for the display, so Luigi suggested she eat her after-dinner mints on the way.

When Stella saw children with sparklers, she couldn't help remembering the times John had taken her and his sister to watch a display, insisting they wore mittens and hold the sparklers at arm's length while he lit them. Still, she was a grown up now and couldn't keep acting like a kid.

Stella spotted Daphne and John, hidden under hats and scarves, walking towards them in the flickering light of the huge bonfire.

"Happy birthday, mate," Daphne yelled, just before she was close enough.

The girls hugged each other.

"I thought you had to work tonight?" Stella said.

"I did, but when Luigi heard how we always watch fireworks together on your birthday he arranged a stand in for a couple of hours. I knew you'd need me. Blokes are rubbish about this sort of thing, always oohing when they should be aahing," Daphne said.

"There's a difference?" John asked.

"See what I mean?" Daphne giggled.

Luigi nodded to John, who held up two pairs of woolly mittens. Luigi produced a pack of sparklers from the deep pockets of his Abercrombie coat and gave the girls two each.

"Men have some uses," he said.

The men stood shaking their heads, while the girls squealed and waved their fireworks around to write their names.

As Stella walked home from work later that week, John drove past in a police car. He pulled into a bus stop and wound down the window.

"Hi, Stella. OK?"

"Yes, fine," she snapped before realising she could do with an ally if she were to sort out Daphne's love life. "I hope you and Daphne are too?"

"Yes, I'm working hard and so is Daphne."

"Too hard if you ask me. She should get away from that restaurant and have some fun occasionally."

"Actually, I agree with you. Do you suppose there's anything we can do about it?"

She was slightly surprised to hear him say that, but not as surprised as he was going to be.

"I don't know... Do you have time for a cup of tea or something while we discuss it?" She gave him her sweetest smile and the subtlest flutter of her eyelashes.

She managed to hide her amusement at his reaction, but didn't do so well hiding her own alarm when he politely accepted.

As Stella filled the kettle John checked the locks on her windows. Stella bit her lip. He was on duty and just trying to be helpful.

"Sorry, Stella," he said when he turned to see her watching him. "I'm not just trying to be bossy. There have been more break-ins at the homes of women living alone. Whoever is doing it is probably going to keep doing it until we catch him."

She managed a smile. He was annoying, but she knew he wouldn't want her to be burgled or worse. Maybe the burglar watched her flat and knew she was the only person living in the building. Stella shuddered, remembering the still empty flat below her and the creepy bloke in the donkey jacket she'd occasionally seen outside. For a moment she considered mentioning him to John, but decided against it. John might decide to stake-out her flat for the rest of her life.

"Oh and I think I owe you an apology," John said.

"You do?" This would be a first.

"Mum and Dad's anniversary when I was rude because you were late."

She nodded to show she remembered.

"I'd seen those boys just before I finished work and guessed they'd been drinking but because I didn't want to be late I didn't do anything other than ask a colleague to keep an eye on them. If it's any consolation he did and gave them a verbal warning and the shop that supplied them with drink is being prosecuted. They were only fourteen."

"And you're telling me this now, because...?"

"I know I should have said something before but... I don't know. Every conversation we have seems to go wrong doesn't it?"

It did, but maybe if they both made an effort they could learn to get along.

"Why don't you go and sit down?" she suggested.

As he moved toward the living room, Stella set out mugs and dropped in teabags.

"Yuck! What did this die of?" John called.

"What?" Stella asked, rushing in. She hoped Thirteen wasn't spilling his stuffing over the carpet.

John was holding one of her pink fluffy slippers. Or at least what had been a pink fluffy slipper when she'd bought the pair two years previously. Now it was a shapeless piece of bald cloth.

"That's not dead. It's just had a hard life. They're still comfortable."

To distract him from the state of her footwear, Stella explained her theory of Daphne hankering after a mystery Mr Perfect.

"You could be right. Any idea who he could be?" John said.

"No, but he'd have to be better than that Goth guy she went out with. Remember him?"

"Yes, but not as well as I remember the look on our parents' faces when she first brought him home."

They giggled together over past relationships enjoyed or endured by Daphne, John and Stella. They even managed a few careful references to their own ill-fated relationship without falling out. Chatting to John was almost as good as laughing over the past with Daphne.

"Oh John, I haven't made you that cup of tea. I'll put the kettle back on."

"Thanks, Stella, but I think I'd better get back to work." He glanced at his watch. "Good grief, I have to go."

He rushed off so quickly that Stella ran through the last part of their conversation to see if she'd said anything to annoy him. She couldn't think of anything and when the intercom buzzed, thought he was playing some bizarre joke on her.

"Luigi!" she said as she let him in. "This is a surprise."

"I saw a police car outside and wondered if everything was all right?"

"Oh yes, it was just John."

"Why did he come?"

"Just for a chat."

"He was here for a long time."

"No, just for a chat."

When she noticed the time was just after seven thirty, she didn't know if she was more surprised she'd spent two hours chatting with John, or that Luigi had noticed and come over for an explanation.

"He is like family to you?" Luigi asked.

"That's right. Have you got time for coffee, or do you have to get back to Trio?"

"I would like to stay a while, but not to drink coffee." His smile made her heart beat faster. "Wait just a moment, I will return."

In less than fifteen minutes he was back, carrying a bottle of sparkling wine. "We will drink this. Stella, I have very good news for you."

She waited impatiently while he set out glasses and fiddled about pouring the wine.

"To us," he said and raised his glass.

"To us," Stella repeated and took a sip. "So what's the good news?"

"We are going to Italy."

"We are?"

"Yes. From November twelfth until the first of December."

"What do you mean? That's less than a week away." It sounded as though he'd made plans already. Her hand clenched the stem of the glass so tightly she put it down through fear of breaking it.

"I have spoken to Mr Clover and told him you will be away." Luigi produced an envelope from his pocket. "Here are the tickets. You have a few days to pack. We shall be staying with my family, who are interested to meet you, but also touring so you will see Pisa and Venice..."

"You've done what?" Just because everyone he met seemed to be instantly charmed by him didn't mean he could control their lives. Even when she was eight years old and living in the children's home nobody had made arrangements for her without at least having the courtesy to mention them to her first.

"It's all right," Luigi said.

It wasn't. He knew she didn't understand families, so why was he so keen for her to meet his? What if they didn't get on, or even worse what if they did? Stella couldn't cope with being welcomed into a family she might eventually lose.

"It is all right. I have arranged everything."

"Not everything. You forgot to check that I wanted to go."

"But of course you do."

"There's no 'of course' about it. You're nowhere near as irresistible as you think you are. It's one thing to take me to some arty film or poncey art gallery that you think I might like, it's quite another to expect me to come away with you for two weeks doing whatever you want me to."

"I think you may have the wrong idea. I've booked separate rooms and..."

"No. You're the one that's got the wrong idea. I think you'd better go."

Stella was still shaking with anger when she heard the street door slam. She gulped down her drink. It didn't improve her mood, but she poured herself another. Long before the second glass was empty she was crying. What on earth was wrong with her? She'd told Daphne she wanted a serious relationship and she loved the sound of Italy, so why weren't her tears ones of joy?

"What's going on?" Daphne demanded as she let herself into Stella's flat. "I haven't seen you all week, Luigi has been in a terrible mood for days and changes the subject if I mention you."

"We've split up. He wanted me to go to Italy with him."

"You don't dump a man for that," Daphne said.

"No, but he'd bought the tickets before asking me and arranged for me to have time off work, had the whole itinerary worked out, just assuming I'd go along with it. He's going tomorrow; I'm not."

"I knew about the trip. I'd have said something, but I thought it would be a lovely surprise. You get on so well with him and you said Italy sounds nice. I thought it was perfect."

That was the problem.

"Too perfect. It's exactly like that gypsy said."

"Hang on a minute! You're not going because Rosie-Lee said you would? If I refused to go on a holiday because some fake fortune teller told me not to then you'd say I was being daft."

"Yes, of course I would," Stella said.

"You're being just as daft to not go because Rosie-Lee said you should."

"I am not." Was that true, she wondered.

"Come on, what did Luigi do that was so wrong?"

Stella couldn't come up with an answer she thought would convince Daphne. In fact she was having trouble coming up with one to convince herself. Luigi had meant it to be the lovely surprise Daphne assumed it would be. Maybe she'd over-reacted.

That night, Stella packed her case and set her alarm for an early start. Luigi would be too tired for an emotional reunion after Saturday night in Trio; she'd surprise him in the morning.

Leaping out of bed as soon as the alarm woke her, Stella showered and dressed in record time. Without stopping even for coffee, she ran down the street through the rain to Luigi's flat. He was going to be so pleased to see her and hear she'd changed her mind about the trip. She'd changed her mind about him too: he wasn't manipulative, he was simply trying to make her happy.

Luigi didn't look as pleased to see her as she'd imagined he would. There were bags under his eyes and he leant on the door frame as though for support. Poor man must have been even more upset by their break-up than she'd realised. She moved closer to offer him a kiss but he stepped aside. Behind him, Stella saw two sets of luggage in his hallway and a leggy blonde, damp from the shower, wrapped in his dressing gown.

Chapter Eight

After running home again, Stella hurled her suitcase into a corner and herself onto her bed. She wasn't sure if she was crying or laughing, but she knew she wanted to share her experience with Daphne.

"Hiya. Are you already at the airport?" Daphne said as she answered Stella's call.

Stella explained she'd arrived at Luigi's flat to find a blonde with a suitcase full of clothes, none of which she was wearing.

"I'm sure there's a simple explanation, maybe she got caught in the rain?" Daphne suggested.

"There's an explanation all right. After I said I wasn't going to Italy, he called an ex-girlfriend and invited her. Except I suppose she's not the ex any more; I am."

"You dumped him, remember."

"Yes, one week ago! And you told me to go on the holiday."

"Yeah. Sorry, bad call. You need serious retail therapy. I'll be there in fifteen minutes."

As they tried on shoes, Daphne said. "I should have checked your horoscope yesterday; it said not to reverse a decision."

"Great, you checked that after I got my heart broken."

"I'm sorry, Stella; I thought you were OK about it. Is your heart really broken?"

"It will be if these aren't available in a wide fitting," Stella said, easing a strappy red sandal off her foot.

"So you're really OK?"

"Course I am. I didn't half feel an idiot though, stood there with my mouth open and my suitcase in my hand." Stella re-enacted the scene.

Daphne giggled.

Stella tried to pout, but gave in and grinned. She picked up a bag to match the sandals. "For once, I agree with your horoscopes; I shouldn't have changed my mind about going away with Luigi. He's fun and generous and all that, but..." Stella shrugged.

"Yeah, sorry mate."

"It's not your fault."

"It is a bit. I introduced you and..."

"OK, you win; it's all your fault. Buy me a coffee and cake and I'll forgive you."

Daphne bought fresh cream apple turnovers to go with their drinks. "This should cheer you up, but if it doesn't put a smile on your face, I'll start telling you John's jokes."

"No, Daphne, that'd be cruel. I'm happy, really, really happy. Honestly."

"He told me one the other day about a policeman and a kitten stuck up a tree..."

"Look at this grin, Daffers. Do I look like a woman wallowing in memories and self pity?"

"No, you don't look like that. You look crazy, but not sad."

"That's because I'm not." She was a bit sad, but that was more because she was without a boyfriend than because she was pining for Luigi. Deep down she'd never really expected their relationship to work out and what had hurt was simply the proof that he was more than willing to have a normal relationship with another girl. It was just Stella who wasn't proper girlfriend material. "It wasn't real. Do you know what I mean, Daffs? As though we were acting in a film or something."

"You did look like the perfect couple and he's so charming."

"Yes, he's charming all right. Everyone falls for him; me, you, that blonde, even your impossible to please brother. I fell for him, but... I don't know." No use worrying now it was over. Stella ended the conversation by taking a big bite of her cake.

Daphne swiftly moved a plate under Stella's chin in time to catch the cream and tangy apple as it oozed from the sugar encrusted pastry. They were quiet until both cakes were just a memory.

"Do you remember your first kiss?" Daphne asked.

"Yes, it was raining and we'd just left the bowling alley..."

"Luigi took you bowling? I wouldn't have thought it was his style."

"Oh, no not Luigi. I thought you were still talking about... er, I thought you meant my first kiss ever."

"Wasn't that my brother?"

"It was. And he was the first boy I ever had a horrible break-up with, no thanks to you."

"It wasn't that horrible and anyway, you're friends now, aren't you?"

"I wouldn't say we're friends exactly. Oh Daphne, it was horrible. He thought I was manipulating him so that I'd be part of your family."

"He didn't."

"Did too. After he'd heard us planning that I'd marry him and we'd be sisters. You must remember."

"Yes, I remember. Once he'd got over being annoyed with you, he decided it was all my fault. He didn't talk to me for weeks."

Stella grinned. "I don't blame him. It was all your fault."

"Thanks, mate."

Stella allowed herself to stay in bed, cuddling Thirteen and wallowing in self pity, on Sunday morning. She remembered every broken relationship she'd been involved in, from the mother she knew little about, every foster family she no longer contacted to her latest boyfriend who'd found a replacement for her before she'd had a chance to miss him.

It was no use, she couldn't even get properly miserable. Her mother probably gave her up in the belief it was the best thing for her; her foster families sent occasional cards and would no doubt be pleased to hear from her if she were to contact them; and Luigi hadn't broken her heart because she hadn't given it to him.

Bored with pretending to be miserable, Stella dragged herself out of bed and opened the curtains. The day was sunny and the street full of people. She blinked and grabbed her watch to check she hadn't slept through all of Sunday. She hadn't. The people were there because they'd watched the Remembrance parade. The passing parade was probably what woke her. Thinking of the wounded veterans and those who'd lost friends and loved ones put all thought of her own moping from her head.

Stella thoroughly cleaned her flat and then sat down to write. Fortunately, she had a pack of blank greetings cards. She used four to send cheery notes to the families who'd fostered her, telling them of her nice flat, interesting job and happy life. The knowledge that each person who read her note would smile and be pleased she was doing OK made her happy, so why were tears now trickling down her face?

"Good morning, Stella," Mr Clover said as she arrived for work on Monday. "I wasn't expecting to see you today. I thought you were going to Italy."

Of course he'd thought the trip was to be a wonderful surprise so they'd not discussed it or Stella's decision not to go or her subsequent change of heart.

"So did Luigi, but he was wrong. I don't like having my life organised for me." She walked past Mr Clover, switched on the till and started rearranging items on the counter.

"I am sorry for my part..."

"Don't worry, I'm not blaming you. It seems that everyone except me thought it was a brilliant idea and that I'd love to go to Italy. Actually, I would, but not with Luigi to meet his parents, it wasn't that sort of relationship. I liked him a lot, but I didn't think it was serious for either of us and then, well I don't know what he was thinking. It's not any sort of relationship now; we've split up. He had a blonde in his flat, can you believe that? So I've come in to work instead because I didn't know what else to do."

"Oh."

Poor Mr Clover looked alarmed. Stella wasn't sure if that was because she'd raised her voice and was gesturing wildly, or because she was clutching the pruning knife. She got her answer when she put down the knife and heard his sigh of relief.

"So, if it's all right with you, I'll cancel the rest of the time off Luigi asked you to book and come in to work this week. I think I'd rather be busy than sat moping at home."

"Yes, of course."

"Can I have another go doing a window display? That might cheer me up."

"Yes, yes. Please do."

After Mr Clover fled to the safety of the tiny kitchen at the back of the shop, Stella noticed last week's window display had already been cleared. The space was draped with a plain white sheet and strewn with paper poppies. Stella went outside to look at it properly.

Although simple, the window must have looked perfect when the remembrance parade passed by yesterday morning. The town was going to be a duller place when Mr Clover retired.

"Please come," Daphne pleaded.

She'd invited Stella to Sunday lunch at Trio on both weekends since Luigi's return from Italy, but Stella had so far refused.

"I've got something to celebrate and it won't be the same without you," Daphne coaxed.

"It doesn't seem right any more."

"That's what you said last week, but Luigi really wants you to come. Please."

"Have you two been talking about me?" Stella demanded.

"A bit. He told me he'd written to his mother saying how well his restaurant was doing and promised to bring a girl home. His mum would have worried if he'd arrived alone after you dumped him and I was right about that blonde having got caught in the rain."

"That's fine then, naturally anybody having been caught in the rain would wander round a flat wearing a skimpy towel."

"If they needed a hot shower to warm up they might and anyway, you said it was a dressing gown, not just a towel."

"I still think it's a pretty feeble excuse."

"I don't think so, not the way he's explained it to me, but it doesn't really matter anyway as you're completely over him."

"True."

"We've got fresh artichokes in and I'm making that lamb dish you like and I'll let you choose the dessert."

"That's bribery! OK, I'll come but for you, not for him."

At lunch, Luigi had the cheek to welcome her as though they were, and had only ever been, just good friends. He didn't look the slightest bit guilty or apologetic. Worse still, she couldn't persuade herself that he should.

John arrived just moments after Stella. She kissed him, told him loudly and enthusiastically how pleased she was to see him and sat next to him. John looked surprised. Luigi didn't appear to notice.

Before dessert was served, Luigi announced he was expanding his business and opening a new restaurant, to be called Quattro, in the next town. As a result, he was promoting key staff, Daphne included. Alberto, the current head chef at Trio would move to Quattro and Daphne was to take over his role at Trio.

"That's brilliant, Daphne. I'm so proud of you," Stella said as she hugged her friend.

There was an excited gabble of voices as everyone sucked up to Luigi, thanking him and promising not to let him down. Stella couldn't understand the fuss; he'd only offered them slightly better jobs for heaven's sake.

"To celebrate, I'd like to offer a glass of my latest cocktail," Luigi said holding up his frosted glass jug.

"It better not be a Depraved Daphne," John muttered into Stella's ear.

"A what?" she whispered back.

"Remember the Sparkling Stella? This cocktail lark seems to be a ploy of his when, er, you know."

Stella wasn't sure she did know, but as it clearly wasn't a compliment of Luigi, she grinned at John. "I thought you liked him?"

"I do, but he's a bit much sometimes."

"Please try a 'Jocular John'," Luigi said as he poured clear red liquid onto tall glasses of crushed ice.

John blushed the colour of the drink. Daphne felt her face must be turning a similar shade with the effort of not laughing.

"I remember how John doesn't drink the cocktails because of driving," Luigi said. "This is without alcohol and I intend to offer it free to drivers."

"Good idea, Luigi," John said. "Anything encouraging people not to drink and drive gets my vote." He took a sip of the drink. "Delicious... and I'm not joking."

Stella was suddenly the only one not laughing. Probably because she was the only one not in love with flipping Luigi. All she wanted to do was get home, hug her stuffed panther and forget about irritating, double-crossing men.

Daphne must have noticed her lack of enthusiasm. "What's up, mate?"

"Sorry, too much garlic bread. Great news about your promotion. Come round later for a coffee and tell me all about it."

When Daphne did just that, she said how wonderful Luigi was to work for. "He really makes me feel I'm capable of running the kitchen and listens to my suggestions and he's so thoughtful. He's there to help when I need it, but he doesn't interfere constantly."

While the kettle boiled, Stella remembered how on a date Luigi had let her try rowing the boat, occasionally putting his hands over hers and encouraging her to pull more strongly with one arm or the other, without once pointing out her steering would have caused them to run aground or get tangled in reeds. "I wish my boss was like that. Mr Clover hardly trusts me with a bouquet, much less give me a chance to prove I'm capable of running the shop in his absence."

"Make him, and make me that coffee you promised."

Stella made the drinks and was about to ask for suggestions on getting her boss to appreciate her when she realised Daphne was still talking about Luigi.

"He's great fun, too. I know his sense of humour isn't as relaxed as John's, but he can still make me laugh."

Daphne wasn't usually heartless. She wouldn't be tormenting Stella with the attributes of a boyfriend she no longer had without a good reason. "You're trying to get us back together?" Stella asked.

"No, honestly I'm not."

"Really? So why are you so keen to convince me he's such a great bloke, just sadly misunderstood?"

"He's my boss and I..."

"I'm sure he's fine as a boss, he's just a lousy boyfriend. Anyway, enough about him. What are we going to wear for our double date with Dracula?"

"Something that's easy to take off, of course," Daphne replied to their standing joke about blood donation. "Hey, maybe that's what the fortune teller meant about you saving my life?"

"You're doing it again."

"What?" Daphne demanded.

"Twisting anything that happens to make it fit either your horoscope or what gypsy Rosie-Lee said."

"And you're twisting it so it doesn't and making sure none of it comes true."

"I am not." What she had been doing was twisting the subject away from Luigi. "If you start choking to death on that biscuit, I'll call an ambulance even though she said I'd save your life, and if a gorgeous, dark hunk asks me out, then believe me I'll accept my fate and say yes."

"Oh good." Daphne smirked.

"I've just been manoeuvred into something, haven't I?"

"Yes." Daphne pretended to be worried and gulped her coffee.

"Come on, what is it? It better not be an attempt to get me back with Luigi. I'm not interested."

"It isn't. Actually it's a way to prove that you're completely over him."

"OK, count me in."

"He's having a big Christmas party to open Quattro and you're invited. You'll turn up with a tall, dark handsome bloke and he'll see you're sooo over him. Plus the party is going to be great. Fabulous food, cocktails, hand-made chocolates..."

Stella held up a hand. "Tiny snag. Where do I get the gorgeous man from? Last time I looked there wasn't a queue of them trailing around after me."

"All taken care of."

"Taken care of how?" Stella knew her suspicion was showing.

"Trust me."

"Like I did about the lime and vodka jellies, or with the table dancing incident, or over the incredible see-through skirt?"

Daphne gave a wicked grin at the memories and Stella had to dig her fingernails into her palm to stop herself giggling and ruining the indignant tone and expression she was attempting to use.

"Er, no, not like that at all. Stells, I've arranged a date for you and I guarantee you'll be impressed."

"Where did you find him?"

"Just trust me, OK?"

Stella tried to stare Daphne out, but it was obvious her friend wasn't going to back down.

"OK, but I'm following your brother's safe date advice. I'll meet this bloke at the restaurant and book a taxi home."

"I'm sure you can trust him too, but that's still a sensible ides."

The taxi part was. Stella was a little less sure about the rest.

Chapter Nine

Clover's florist's was so quiet Stella envied Daphne her busy job and exciting promotion whereas Stella's career was going nowhere. Daphne only took the job because the fortune teller told her to. Maybe the horoscope in the paper would provide Stella with the motivation to look for a better job? She laughed at herself; she must be bored if she was considering reading that rubbish. To occupy herself, Stella sorted the clutter on Mr Clover's desk. She found Luigi's business card and what appeared to be an order.

"What's this?" she asked her boss.

"He wanted us to supply him with flowers for the tables and arrangements for special occasions. Don't worry, I said we wouldn't do it."

She didn't want to have to suck up to Luigi, but they needed the business.

"We should be doing things like that. It'd be a regular income and maybe we'd get more business from it... " She trailed off as she saw Mr Clover seemed upset. Tact wasn't exactly her strong point, but unless he wanted to make even less money she didn't think it could be because of what she'd said.

"What's wrong?" she asked.

"I'm old, Stella. I can't see as well as I could and..." He bowed his head.

Her impulse was to hug him, but she couldn't; they'd never been on intimate terms. Instead she turned the sign to closed, locked the door and made tea.

"Thank you," he mumbled when she placed the mug before him. He didn't say another word until he'd finished the tea and blown his nose.

"Are you going to close the shop?" Stella asked.

"I don't want to. It's been in my family for generations."

"Then don't." Stella remembered she'd closed it, temporarily, herself. "I'll go and open up again, shall I?" she asked.

Mr Clover nodded.

When Stella returned, he was still hunched in his chair clutching his empty mug. Stella couldn't think of anything to say, so she offered more tea. Mr Clover did manage a slight smile as he accepted the refilled mug.

The ping of the shop bell informed Stella they had a customer. "I'll get it," she said.

Leaning against the counter was an absolute hunk dressed in tight jeans and a leather jacket which looked soft enough to snuggle up to. He was the most gorgeous bloke she'd seen since... well since she was last dreaming her favourite fantasy.

"Can I help?" Stella asked. The chances of him wanting anything other than flowers were slim, but she tried to imply there were lots of things she'd be prepared to help him with.

"I'd like to order some flowers, please."

Wow, he looked even sexier when he grinned at her.

"Of course. Are they for a special occasion?"

"I hope so."

"Everything all right, Stella?" Mr Clover called.

"Yes, fine," she replied. She wasn't sure she really could handle the man in front of her, but she certainly wanted to try.

"I'm hoping to impress an attractive young lady. What would you suggest?"

Just turning up would do it, but she wouldn't mind him taking off his jacket to reveal a tight white T-shirt. Sadly though he was just a customer. In common with all the other attractive men she met through work, this one was buying flowers for someone else. Other than Luigi, Mr Clover was the only man who'd ever given her flowers. Well, there had been one other; John aged thirteen had picked daisies for eleven year old Stella to make daisy chains to wear in a May Day parade. He'd picked them for Daphne too though, so maybe they didn't count. Oh well, back to reality and work.

"Red roses always make a statement," she told Gorgeous Bloke.

"Red roses it is, then." He paid in cash.

Stella grinned. Those flowers weren't for her, but it still made her happy to imagine the effect they'd have on the girl he'd give them too. A couple of seconds fantasising about him putting a rose between his teeth and wanting to make her happy had an effect on her too. There would be another man in her life soon and he'd give her flowers, she was sure. Flowers were important to her and so was her job.

She returned to Mr Clover. "You said you don't want to close the shop?"

"That's right."

"Then don't. We can keep it going. I could do a lot more than fill buckets with water and serve customers."

"You could, but you made it clear when you started here that it was just until you found something better."

"Give me a better job then. I was planning to go to a bigger shop and get management training, but I like working with flowers, the colours and the scents. I've done the windows a few times and I haven't scared the customers away."

"True."

"And I saw it was a good idea to start stocking the herb plants, do you remember?"

"I do. The flowers for Hallowe'en were your suggestion as well. You do seem to have an aptitude for the floristry business."

"So, train me properly and then make me your manager."

"I will think about it," he said. The smile which lit up his eyes told her he'd do more than that.

Between serving customers, Mr Clover and Stella made plans for brightening up the shop and attracting more customers. For a start they could print advertising leaflets for Stella to give out at Luigi's party.

Stella was determined it wasn't just the leaflets which would attract attention. That meant she had to go shopping. A day shopping was maybe not the best start to her management training, but she'd already asked for the day off and booked a hair appointment so trying to find something suitable to wear wasn't going to harm her career.

The red dress was perfect. A girl who had recently split up with a man who'd then humiliated her wouldn't have the nerve to wear it, but a woman who was about to be promoted and was attending her best friend's party on the arm of a stunning, tall, dark, handsome man could carry it off. The low neckline and softly draping material transformed her generous figure into voluptuous curves and complemented her striking dark looks. She already had new strappy sandals in the same vibrant shade as the dress, so just needed the salon to ensure her sometimes unruly hair was tamed into a flowing, glossy wave. Whoever Daphne had arranged to take her to the party was going to be well and truly impressed.

As Stella's hair was blow dried, she flicked through a glossy magazine. It fell open on the horoscope page. Apparently she couldn't see what was right in front of her and would soon face a test of friendship. There wasn't a word about her making a big impression and nothing about her life changing for the better, which just showed what complete rubbish those things were.

Daphne came round to Stella's flat after her lunchtime shift at Trio and found Stella with her hair wrapped in a protective towel and her face smeared with a deep cleansing masque.

"Oh sorry, Stella, did you think it was a fancy dress party? Hallowe'en was ages ago."

"Oi! I had my hair done, but all that hot air made my face shiny, so I'm using one of those clay and lavender things from the beauty parlour next to Clover's. There's some left in the tub, if you want it."

"I probably need it, but I haven't got time; I'll have to go back to work soon, but I needed a break."

"Have a look at my new dress, it's on the bed. That'll wake you up."

Daphne followed her friend's instructions and went into the bedroom.

"Wow! That's fantastic," she called.

"Isn't it? Go and put the kettle on while I take this off, so we can talk properly."

"Be quick then, I really don't have long. I promised Luigi I'd be at Trio in an hour and that was fifteen minutes ago."

Stella splashed water on her face to soften the masque enough for her to speak without flaking.

Daphne's mug was still warm when she left to go back to Trio. Stella had never met anyone so eager to get to work. Maybe there was a dishy new waiter Daphne wanted to keep a close eye on. Yes, that must be the explanation. Daphne was always going on about work and how great it was; her mystery man must work there or somehow be connected with Trio. Stella would keep her eyes peeled during the party.

The only advantage of no social life was that Stella had time for a practice run with her make-up, waxing legs and manicuring hands on the night before the party, so really it didn't take her long to get ready once Daphne left. She finished preening and pampering, inspected herself in the mirror, applied another coat of mascara for luck and caught a bus to Quattro.

Luigi's new restaurant had an ornate brass number four on the door. Had the number of the premises inspired Luigi's naming of his restaurants, or had he selected the buildings deliberately to fit?

"Ah Stella, I'm flattered you're so eager to see me you come early," Luigi said in his strongest accent as he let her in.

"Don't kid yourself, pal; I'm here to see Daphne. I'm only here because she wants me to be and not because you're anyway near as irresistible as you like to think."

"I know. Sorry, I know it is awkward between us and was trying to ease the tension with a joke."

"Oh." She knew he was the one in the wrong, so how had he managed to make her feel as though she'd behaved badly? Maybe he'd decide to carry on where John had left off with that.

"Daphne, Stella is here," Luigi called as he led the way into the kitchen.

Daphne looked up through a cloud of steam. "I'll be there in a minute, I can't leave this just yet."

"OK, Daffs."

"She is very busy, but you sit here," Luigi said as he indicated a wooden stool, "and I will bring you a drink."

Daphne raced over. "Be nice to him, Stella. He's been nervous about this restaurant launch and worried he's upset you and it'd be nice for me if you were friends... Sorry, gotta get back to the stove."

Luigi was soon back with a glass of something pink. After handing it to her, he took a step away and then paused as though not sure if he should talk to her or keep well away. Maybe he really did feel as nervous as Daphne had said.

"Thanks. Luigi, I'm sorry, I didn't mean to be rude earlier; like you said, it's awkward. Thanks for inviting me and... my friend to your party." Embarrassingly, Stella didn't yet know her date's name.

"I'm glad you could come. Friends?"

"Yes, friends." She raised her glass to him and took a sip of the delicious strawberry concoction. She'd have asked what it was called, but Luigi had already gone, leaving her to watch the frantic activity in the kitchen.

"What's happened?" she asked as soon as Daphne felt she could leave the stove.

"Happened where?"

"Here. This place is chaos."

"It's a kitchen; it's what they're like when it's busy. I think everything's pretty much under control now though. You look stunning, by the way."

"Thanks, I've brought my make-up kit, so you soon will too."

"I've just got to glaze these canapés. Talk to me while I do. Once Doug arrives you might not want to chat to me. He's absolutely gorgeous, I promise you."

"Daffers, I'm getting worried about this. This is the second gorgeous bloke you've fixed me up with instead of snaffling for yourself. You haven't gone off men have you?"

"Of course not. Actually there is someone I like, but it's impossible."

"Why? Is he married?"

"No."

"Twelve? Dead? Fictitious?"

"No, no and no. Look don't worry about him, let me tell you about Doug. He really is good looking and he's got a good job. Actually that's how I know him, he's a colleague of John's."

"John's arranged a blind date for me? Daphne, that's not very reassuring."

Daphne laughed. "Don't worry, he's lovely. I picked him and asked him, John had nothing to do with it. Actually he wasn't very happy about it when I told him."

John wouldn't be. Hopefully he hadn't had time to poison his friend's mind against her. She took a breath and reminded herself she intended to get out the habit of always thinking the worst of her friend's brother.

As Stella transformed Daphne from very red faced chef, to slightly red faced party girl, in seven minutes flat she explained about her new role at work.

"Mr Clover is going to train me. I won't just be selling bunches of flowers, I'll be learning to do everything, even helping with the accounts. Trainee manager, that's what I am."

"Brilliant news!"

"Isn't it? I'll be good too, Daffs. He won't regret it. I'm going to try and get us more customers too. Luigi will buy flowers from us, I'm sure, and lots of other places might. I've made up advertising leaflets. I thought maybe I could give some out tonight?"

"Wow, you've been busy. Let's see them."

Stella took the roll of fliers from her handbag.

"Nice. I'll point out people who run businesses so you can hand these out. At least I will if you're not too busy with Doug."

"You think that's likely?"

"Yep. Come on, let's get this party started."

"Daphne, you look wonderful," Luigi enthused as the girls entered the restaurant.

Daphne, Luigi and Alberto, Quattro's new head chef, and the manager stood by the door, reminding Stella of the receiving line at a wedding. Party guests arrived, some in groups of friends, most in couples. No one wanted to speak to her. Luigi might have said he wanted to be friends, but he was doing a fine job of ignoring her. Even Daphne hardly spoke to her as she was busy greeting guests, all of whom she knew. Stella wasn't being fair. Of course Luigi and Daphne had to greet the guests, it was just disappointing to have made the effort to get there early for Daphne's sake and to have bit her lip and been nice to Luigi, only to be left on her own, like an unwanted bridesmaid who had to be asked just to keep the in-laws quiet. It was a relief to see John arrive followed by a tallish, attractive man.

"John, great to see you," she said as she rushed to greet him.

"Er, you too, Stella. That dress is very..."

What was wrong with the bloke? He looked surprised to see her which was ridiculous as he'd brought her date. Even more ridiculous was that instead of wanting to be introduced to her, his mate had wandered off. Maybe she should be worried what was wrong with her; had she spilled her drink down her front or got her skirt tucked into her knickers? A quick glance reassured her everything was clean and where it was supposed to be.

"Where's your friend Doug gone?"

"Sorry, you'll have to make do with me, something came up."

"But he's only just got here."

"No he hasn't."

Did he really have to argue with her about every little thing? "Then who's the bloke who came in with you?"

"No idea, but he seems to be with a pregnant redhead."

Stella glanced behind her and saw he was right. She also saw he wasn't really tall, he'd just seemed so in comparison to John. He wasn't even that attractive. Nothing was going right.

Chapter Ten

"Doug's held up did you say?" Stella demanded.

"He's working."

"Oh really? Did you even ask him, John, or did you think this would be a great chance to humiliate me?"

"What? Why would I do that?"

"You've never liked me have you? You think I'm manipulative, stupid and a bad influence on your sister and..."

"Stella, Doug couldn't come because he'd been called to investigate a burglary. The woman who'd had her house broken into while she slept is eighty-three. She's terrified and he's promised to stay with her until her granddaughter can get there."

"Oh." John might not mean to humiliate her but he'd just managed to do it again.

"Come on, let's get a drink," he said.

Stella nodded.

"How about we ask Luigi to make a pitcher of Sparkling Stella, eh? Remind him of what he's missing."

His grin was so like his sister's Stella couldn't help smiling back.

"Actually," John said, "I'm tempted to ask him to mix something short and potent in honour of your dress. That might take his mind off blonde bimbos."

"You wouldn't."

"I will if you want me too. Daphne said you wanted to make a point to Luigi and I've let you down with Doug and..."

First Luigi, now John, it seemed she was making a habit of misjudging people who had intended to be nice to her. She really should lighten up and enjoy the party.

"Thanks, John. I'm over Luigi really, I am."

"Shame, he's a nice bloke and very generous, but he is a bit full of himself. I was kind of looking forward to winding him up."

Stella remembered she was going to have to try and sweet talk Luigi into buying flowers from her. She wanted him to be perfectly clear it was only his business she was interested in.

"No reason why we shouldn't," Stella said and kissed John's cheek.

"I'm going to have to arrest you."

"For kissing you?"

"No, for stealing my heart."

"That's truly terrible."

"I haven't even started yet. Better get you a drink before I try again though, I wouldn't want you to listen to my patter on an empty stomach."

John returned with drinks and a plate of snacks. He handed her a stuffed olive and took one for himself.

"What do you think my olive's going to say to yours after a couple of drinks?"

"I don't know. Something oily, I suppose?"

John held up his olive and wobbled it over to the one Stella held. "Olive you," he slurred.

John kept her supplied with drinks, insisted the waiting staff brought them at least one of every kind of canapés and snack on offer, as his sister was the chef, and told her funny stories about other party guests.

"Good to see the mayor has got his chain on," he remarked.

"I thought he always wore it at events like this?"

"You'd think so, but not long after he got elected, he left it in the council offices when he went home. He was opening a youth club that night and supposed to wear it, so went back. The council offices were all locked up, except that he noticed he'd left a window open. He was too embarrassed to call anyone out, so tried to get in through the window."

Stella glanced at the mayor's ample frame. "Hope it was a big window?"

"It wasn't, and this was before his diet."

Stella giggled.

"You've guessed it, he got stuck. I had to pull off his trousers and smear him with Vaseline."

"No! Good thing no one saw you, can you imagine the headlines?"

"He could. Poor chap, when I went round the next day to advise him on security for his office, he thought I'd come for a statement. He's always most generous when I collect for the police benevolent fund."

She was sure John exaggerated wildly, but he was so funny it didn't matter. He leant close and touched her face or whispered more corny chat up lines whenever Luigi was in sight. Why had she ever thought John was no fun?

When John headed for the gents, Stella looked round to see if there was anyone else she knew at the party or who she could persuade John to gossip about. A bunch of red roses was presented to her.

"Stella, darling," said the most gorgeous looking bloke Stella had clapped eyes on since... he'd ordered those very roses from her yesterday. He slipped his arm around her waist, pulled her tight and brought his sexy lips close as though about to kiss her.

"Hi, I'm Doug. Hope I'm not overdoing it?"

"Not at all," Stella said. It was then she realised several of the party guests were staring at them. She saw Daphne push Luigi in the direction of the toilets then head towards her.

"I've sent Luigi to delay John, so you can escape," Daphne told Doug.

"I'm not sure I want to escape," Doug said.

His arm was still around Stella who wasn't sure she wanted him to escape either. Actually she was sure she didn't.

"Luigi thinks she's dating John now," Daphne explained.

"Actually, by now he probably thinks I'm two timing him," Stella said.

"And you care what he thinks?" Doug asked.

"Not any more."

"Put my friend down," insisted Daphne.

Doug plucked one long stemmed rose from the bouquet and held it in his teeth whilst he gave the rest of the bouquet to Daphne. He then tucked the single one behind Stella's ear and went in search of a drink. Stella sighed. She was going to have to fantasise a lot more if her day dreams developed a habit of coming true the very next day.

When John returned he said, "Luigi was acting very weird. He started asking me all kinds of random questions in the gents."

"Daphne sent him to delay you when Doug turned up."

"Doug's here? What do you want to do now, Stella?"

"Enjoy the party," Stella said.

"Good plan."

"I'll just go and check that the panna cotta are OK and I'll be right with you." Daphne disappeared back into the kitchen, collecting Luigi on her way.

Doug returned with drinks for himself and Stella.

"You're too late, mate," John informed him. "When you didn't show, Stella decided she was better off with me."

"No, mate. I think you'll find the girl has better taste than that. What do you say, Stella, shall we make up for lost time?" Doug took her glass from her, handed it and his own to John and led Stella onto the intimate space in the centre of the restaurant which was being used as a dance floor.

Stella found her time was divided between Doug and John, both of whom seemed determined to be more amusing and complimentary than the other.

Daphne did manage to spend a few minutes chatting to her, but each time she was soon called away either by a member of staff or the need to entertain an important guest.

Doug brought Stella a selection of dainty white and dark chocolate Florentines, topped with pistachios and cherries, and tiny truffle filled chocolates shaped like the leaning tower of Pisa.

"I wasn't sure which you'd prefer so I got some of each."

"Good idea, you can't go wrong feeding me anything that's covered in chocolate, but these little white ones with nuts in are my absolute favourite."

"I'll go and see if there are any more left."

The moment Doug disappeared from her left side, John appeared on her right. He was bearing a selection of tiny pizzas shaped into the figure four. Before John could get close enough to offer the snack to Stella, Luigi stepped between them, brandishing a very large pepper grinder.

"Allow me to season your food," he said in the strongest accent Stella had ever heard him use. He made a dramatic performance of applying pepper to the plate, bowed low and vanished.

Stella caught John's glance and they both giggled.

"Is it just me, or is that thing getting bigger?" John asked.

"It is bigger, but I'm not entirely sure that's anything to do with you!"

"Go on, grind me down with your peppery remarks."

"At least I'm not rubbing salt into the wound."

Stella had forgotten how much more attractive John looked when he smiled. She ate her tiny pizza very slowly; she wasn't anxious for John to go away for more and not entirely because she'd already eaten so much.

Daphne joined them. "Sorry to leave you for so long. It's hard work ensuring the waiting staff don't let the mayor go hungry. John, would you get me some water, please?"

"You've done brilliantly, Daffs," Stella said. "The food is absolutely amazing. I don't suppose there will be anything left over, but if there is don't you dare chuck any of it out -

I'll have the lot. It's all fantastic, but I like the tiny white chocolates the best. Love how you used green pistachio nuts and cherries to make Italian flags. Was that your idea?"

"It was. Actually it was inspired by you. I was thinking up ways to make the chocolates appropriate for the party and for the guests. I covered a few in golden foil and arranged one plateful with them on so it looked like the mayor's chain and made sure he was the first to be offered one of them. Actually he was probably the last too, as he ate quite a lot of them."

"Don't blame him, they were delish, but how did I inspire you?" Stella said.

"I just tried to imagine what you'd like best and then realised those ingredients were the colours of the Italian flag. Easy."

"I bet you'd be good at flower arranging."

"Don't you dare suggest that to Luigi; I already have quite enough to do. Anyway, how are you getting on with Doug?" Daphne asked.

"Great, he's a laugh and so is your..."

Before she could finish, Luigi appeared. "I was hoping to persuade you to dance, if you have the time," he said.

Stella glanced behind him hoping to catch the attention of John or Doug.

"Sorry, Luigi, but I promised this one to John," she said.

To save face, Luigi took Daphne's hand instead. When John returned with Daphne's water, Stella dragged him onto the dance floor.

"Maybe now he'll see what a big mistake he made by messing up with you," John said as he held Stella close and moved with the music. Stella didn't know if he meant Luigi was a fool to lose her, a rat to get another girlfriend so quickly or just getting into the part of one of her many admirers. What she did know was that it was fun to dance and flirt with him, and Doug too of course.

"Stella, I'm sorry, but I've had a very long day and have to go," Doug told her.

"Oh yes, John told me about the lady who got burgled."

"Maybe I could see you again?"

"I'd like that," she said.

When Stella and John realised they were the last non-staff guests, they decided they too should leave. They couldn't find either Luigi or Daphne.

"I'll take you home, Stella," John offered as they walked out to wait for the taxi she'd called.

Daphne and Luigi were outside in the cool air, obviously they'd been saying good-bye to important guests.

"It's been great, but I think it's time we went," John said. "Do you want a lift home, Daphne?"

"I'm going to stay here for a while. Don't worry, John, Luigi promised to make sure I get home safely."

John didn't look particularly reassured, even when Daphne explained he hadn't been drinking. Daphne ignored him and went back inside.

Stella slipped her arm round John's waist, leant close to his ear, but not so close Luigi wouldn't hear her stage whisper, "Oh good, it looks like it's just us then."

Luigi said goodnight and returned to the restaurant as though he hadn't noticed. Sure that he'd glance out as he closed the door, Stella kissed John. He pulled her tight. He really was a great kisser.

"Would you like a raisin?" John asked on the way to her home.

"Er, no thanks." What was he on about? He'd seen how much she'd eaten so couldn't possibly think she was hungry.

"Oh, how about a date?"

"Oh!" For a moment she thought he meant it. Then realised, as he'd just fixed her up with his mate, it had to be another of his dodgy jokes.

"Very good. You should try that one for real, it might actually work."

"Really, do you fancy..."

"Obviously it'd depend who you asked."

John barely pecked her on the cheek after waiting until she'd opened her door and switched on the lights. Thank goodness she'd realised in time that he was joking about the date. It'd have been way too embarrassing for both of them if she'd said yes. Not that she would have done, obviously.

Chapter Eleven

Sunday wasn't any fun. Her head hurt for one thing. That was Luigi's fault; how was a girl supposed to know what was in those cocktails of his? Two paracetamol washed down with a glass of grapefruit juice, a long shower and second glass of grapefruit helped a bit with the pain, but not Stella's mood. Her memory was a little hazy too. Doug was supposed to have been her date, but he'd turned up late and put her in the embarrassing situation of having to be nice to John. Men! To be fair, Doug had made a determined effort to make up for lost time and John had really helped her give Luigi the message she was well and truly over him. But that had all been before Doug left, never to be heard of again, and John flounced off in a huff after escorting her home.

The weather wasn't helping either. It was cold and damp. The weather forecast, if she could bear to listen, would probably repeat the news that it was very mild for the time of year. Perhaps it was mild for December, but it was still cold. A nice bright frost she could handle; lots of layers and bright woolly accessories and she was set. Constant drizzle, from clouds that seemed to be just a few feet above her head and sinking fast, couldn't be avoided unless she stayed indoors all day.

It wasn't just men and the weather that were letting her down; she'd only had her new mobile a few weeks and either it was already broken or Daphne hadn't called to chat about the party and Doug hadn't called to invite her out. She wasn't sure which was most annoying.

Stella checked her watch and discovered it was too late to try calling Daphne before she started work as she'd already be there kneading bread rolls or whatever she did to get ready. There was to be no staff lunch as they'd all be busy clearing up or recovering from the party, so Stella would have to fend for herself all weekend. She sent Daphne a text asking her to call when she finished cooking lunch and then set about burning herself some cheese on toast.

By the time Daphne rang, Stella had worked herself into a fit of depression.

"I thought Christmas was going to be fun, but it's going to be awful. I'll be all on my own and I'll be so lonely..."

"Oh dear, your head hurts and Doug hasn't rung?" Daphne guessed.

"Well, yes, I mean no, he hasn't, but..."

"Put the kettle on, I'll be round in a few minutes. Have a glass of water while you wait, you're probably dehydrated."

Stella drank the water. She didn't believe she'd had enough alcohol the night before to still be affected, but she did believe Daphne would nag her if she didn't follow her advice.

"So, what's up?" Daphne asked once they were both settled on the sofa with mugs of tea.

"Nothing is working out how I hoped." Stella knew she sounded like a whinging child, but she couldn't help it.

"What were you hoping for?"

"I thought Christmas was going to be fun, this year. I was sure Doug liked me and would ask me out again, I thought I'd get to spend time with you now we're both single and as John's been friendly lately, I thought I'd be able to spend Christmas with your family again this year. None of that is working out; you're busier than ever, Doug hasn't called, I've somehow upset John again and I don't suppose your parents will want a misery like me hanging around anyway. All I wanted was a nice boyfriend and a family, was that too much to ask?"

"No, love," Daphne said as she put her arm around Stella.

"I've been lucky with the foster families I've stayed with. They were all kind to me and we've kept in touch with Christmas cards and stuff, but it isn't the same as a real flesh and blood family."

"I know. I'm lucky, I've got John and my parents and a whole host of aunts, uncles and cousins, who I know will always be on my side. I can't imagine what it's like not to have that. When I was a kid, I so wanted you to be part of my family."

"Yeah and look where that got us."

Daphne grimaced. "OK, fixing you up with John and letting him hear our plans for the two of you to get married just so you'd be my sister wasn't my best ever move."

"No, but he got over it eventually. I never did work out how, even when he knew it was your idea, he forgave you and not me."

"Because I'm his sister." Daphne shrugged.

"Yeah, I guess. I'm not ever going to understand, am I?"

"Stella, I didn't mean to..."

"It's OK. I bet if I did have a sister we wouldn't have got on as well as you and I do."

"No one gets on as well as we do."

"Not with me anyway. I fall out with everybody, even gorgeous generous Italians who were just trying to give me what they thought I wanted. You know, I always knew Luigi wasn't the man for me. If I shared your superstitious nature, I'd have said it wasn't my destiny to be with him."

"Actually, I think you're right about that one. I so wanted the fortune teller to be right, I couldn't see what should have been obvious from the start."

"So, no tall dark handsome man for me?"

"Not at the moment. Don't worry though, you've got me still," Daphne reassured her, "and my family. They'd love you to come for Christmas lunch."

"Ask them first."

"OK, but they'll say yes."

Stella nodded. She too was sure they'd agree. Daphne's parents had always been very kind to her, including her in family activities and taking her with them on their annual beach holiday.

"You are OK, really?" Daphne asked as she prepared to leave.

"Yeah."

It was true, Stella realised. Her head felt better and the phone worked; things weren't as bad as she thought. Outside it was damp and dark, but she had a waterproof coat and a bobble hat. A brisk walk around the block might perk her up.

As the street was nearly empty, even though it wasn't yet six o'clock, Stella didn't need to worry too much about how she looked so wore her flowery wellington boots, brightest gloves and three different scarves, none of which went with the hat. Hopefully if she was spotted, it would be by a stranger who'd be amused by her appearance. She probably wasn't the only person who needed cheering up.

Stella passed two elderly ladies pulling shopping trolleys, both of whom returned her smile. Apart from them, she had the High Street to herself. It seemed as though something was missing and she looked carefully at the shop fronts and street lights, expecting to notice a change. When a builder's van passed, Stella realised she'd half expected to see the bloke in a donkey jacket who was often hanging around near her door. She wasn't sorry he wasn't about; he gave her the creeps.

After a while, Stella heard music and found herself walking towards it. Outside the library a crowd had gathered around a brass band playing 'Silent Night'. The crowd were singing. An elderly couple gestured for her to join them. The man held a paper booklet so both Stella and his wife could read the words.

"Come on, sing up," he said.

"Thanks, but I'd better just listen. My singing is terrible."

"Don't you worry about that dear," his wife said. "Neither of us can hold a tune, truth be told. That's why we stand at the back."

They sounded fine to Stella, but she knew she wasn't much of a judge. They didn't wince when she joined in the last verse, so perhaps the lady was right. Her new friends chatted enthusiastically to her as the band prepared for each song. By the time they'd worked their way through 'In the Bleak Midwinter', 'The Holly and the Ivy' and 'God Rest Ye Merry Gentlemen' Stella had learnt the names and occupations of each of their children and children-in-law, plus the names of the seven grandchildren and knew what gift each and every one of them was to receive for Christmas.

"That's a lot of wrapping," Stella said.

"And a lot of cooking. They're all coming to us for Christmas this year," the lady said.

Stella couldn't help smiling at her excitement. "Good grief. You must have a big house."

"No, but the neighbours are lending us their caravan and Daniel, our eldest, has got one of those fancy motor home things, so I guess we'll manage somehow."

"I hope you all have a lovely time," Stella said. She was grateful the band chose that moment to start 'Good King Wenceslas' before they could ask about her family, as she didn't want to have to explain to them that she was an orphan.

When they did get around to asking, she was ready; or at least she thought she was.

"We're going to John's parents for the day. All the family will be there, I'm really looking forward to it."

Although she had no idea why she'd blurted that out, even she could see it would only confuse the issue if she were to explain she'd only be there because of his sister.

Daphne was right, her family made Stella feel welcome.

"We're so glad you were able to come," Daphne's mum gushed as though she was convinced Stella had a hectic social life she'd put on hold just for them. She'd had the knack of making Stella feel special from the first time she'd filled in a mountain of paperwork so Stella could spend Christmas with her friend rather than in a children's home.

Even John seemed pleased to see her and kissed her cheek as she arrived. She kissed his in return. Soon everyone was kissing everyone else as they gave and received silly presents. Several people gave Daphne a wooden spoon. Her thanks were like Oscar acceptance speeches by the time she'd unwrapped the fifth one. She presented everyone with beautiful boxes of handmade chocolates, each carefully made into their first initial and decorated with their favourite fruit, nuts or other sweet topping.

John kissed Stella again as she handed him the marvellously stylish musical socks she'd chosen for him. They played the kind of tune that a small child without much practise might have managed on a xylophone and featured slightly deformed reindeers with 3D antlers and red pom-poms for noses. Personally she thought the manufacturers had overdone it with the scratchy looking tinsel at the top, but John seemed delighted and immediately put them on.

Stella kissed him again after she'd opened his gift to her. If he'd obeyed the family rule of no more than £5 per person, he'd got a marvellous deal on her pink fluffy slippers. How sweet of him to remember, even if he did entertain everyone to a wildly exaggerated tale about her old ones attacking him when she'd almost made him a cup of tea in her flat.

After a superb lunch cooked by Daphne's uncle Eric with the aid of a constant supply of instructions from Daphne and a constant supply of sherry from Daphne's dad, they all collapsed onto the sofa, chairs and the floor to watch a film. By the time it finished, half the audience were asleep. Stella was awake, but felt as though she were dreaming. She'd eaten a wonderful meal, was comfortably settled in a warm room and surrounded by a loving family; that was pretty much all she'd ever wanted from life. If she was being picky, she'd need a good man by her side to complete the fantasy. She glanced down at John who was leaning against her chair. No getting away from it, he was a good man. Kind, responsible and a friend to her even though they frequently irritated each other.

Stella allowed herself to imagine how things might have been if she and John had become a proper couple. Much like this she supposed, except he'd be sitting even closer with his arm around her and she'd be leaning against him. Daphne's gran interrupted these pleasant thoughts to announce she'd like to take a short walk and wanted John and Stella to come with her.

"I worry about slipping, but I'll feel safe if I can hold on to you two."

As the three of them walked slowly to the end of the street, Gran told them tall tales of pranks she and her sisters got up to at Christmas. Stella laughed so hard at her account of the vicar talking to a snowman they'd built between the pub and the vicarage that she was sure Gran was supporting her rather than the other way around.

"I wish it really would snow," Stella said. "There's something magical about a white Christmas, don't you think?"

"Yes. These days I'm wary of ice and snow in case I fall, but it does look pretty, especially in the countryside."

"We could walk back through the park and you two romantics can use your imagination to pretend you're in a snowstorm in the countryside," John said.

He led them across the playing field where he, Daphne and Stella had teamed up to play cricket and rounders against other children in the summer holidays. They passed the swings and roundabouts they'd often played on and frequently fallen off. When they reached an avenue of trees, John gently detached his arm from his grandmother's grasp.

"The council have done a good job with their salt. Even here where there's still frost on the trees, the path isn't slippery," Gran said.

"Good job, or we'd be in danger of having to carry John home," Stella said.

They both laughed as they watched John run ahead, leaping into the air at every other step to shake the bare branches above his head.

"What is that boy doing?" Gran asked.

"He's making it snow!"

John had loosened the thick hoar frost clinging to the trees allowing tiny ice crystals to drift down onto Stella and Gran.

"How pretty," Stella said.

"And to think he said we were the romantics," Gran said. During the rest of the walk, she told them more stories of Christmas adventures she'd enjoyed during her childhood. In the porch, the old lady stopped and said she thought it really would snow.

"I can't see it, Gran," John said.

"Don't suppose you can, lad. You can't see what's plain as the nose on your face half the time, but you can see that up there, I expect?" She jabbed her thumb upwards before letting go of both of them and taking herself into the house, all trace of her earlier frailty vanished.

John and Stella looked into the roof of the porch to see a large bunch of mistletoe, decorated with a huge tartan bow.

"That wasn't there earlier," John said.

As she lowered her head from the greenery and berries it seemed that John was standing much closer than when she'd looked up. "Surely your gran didn't shin up there?" she asked without moving away.

"I wouldn't put it past her. We'd better not rush back in too quickly. Once she's got an idea in her head, she doesn't give up until she gets what she wants."

"What is it she wants?" Stella asked, even though it seemed pretty clear that Daphne must have inherited her matchmaking urge from her grandmother.

"Come on, Stella, isn't it obvious?"

John pulled her into his arms and bent his head toward her. She lifted hers, to meet his kiss. Christmas is no time to disappoint sweet old ladies. It was no time to disappoint Stella either. John's kiss was perfect; warm and so gentle it wouldn't shake her out of her post dinner dream. The way he was holding her felt pretty nice too.

"Uncle John, what are you doing to Stella?" demanded a squeaky voice.

Stella awoke immediately and discovered she really was standing in the porch with John's arms around her. Obviously John's cousin had arrived with her children during their walk as one of them was now peering out at them through the letter box.

"Do we explain, or go in?" John asked.

As Stella was incapable of understanding what had just happened, let alone explain to a small child, they went in. Every seat, except a large beanbag, was taken. Stella and John just about managed to balance on it, although John had to put his arm around Stella to stop her slithering off.

Later, John drove her home. Stella didn't know if she were disappointed or relieved when the children insisted on accompanying them. Making the most of the situation, she enthusiastically joined in with their carol singing during the drive. John sang too, occasionally reaching down to switch on his socks as an accompaniment.

The children had been brought up to expect kisses when saying goodnight and each dampened her cheek before telling Uncle John to do the same. He'd hardly got started before they dragged him away again.

As they descended the stairs from her flat, she heard one of the children say, "Is Stella your girlfriend?"

It was cold in Stella's flat after the warmth of a family Christmas, so she wore her new furry slippers to bed and wondered what answer he gave.

Chapter Twelve

"What do you think of these?" Daphne asked two days after Christmas. She lifted her hair to give Stella a better view of the string of sparkling crystals dangling from her ears. At the end of each was a tiny green four leafed clover.

"They're so pretty! How's this for a coincidence, I won a bottle of drink just that colour. Want to try it?"

"Go on then, just a small one. We've got lots of bookings tonight and I don't want to fall asleep in the zabaglione."

"I'll make it a really tiny one if you're going to have to say that."

"Luckily I find it easy to pronounce. Or at least I would if..."

"If what?"

"If my mouth wasn't so dry."

"All right, I can take a hint."

Stella grabbed the bottle and two shot glasses. She poured a splash into each. "I'm not sure it's going to be very nice. It was a raffle prize and a box of tissues and a handmade tea cosy were chosen before this."

Daphne held her glass up to her ear.

"Perfect match. Where did you get them?"

"Luigi gave them to me. He says I've brought luck to him since I've been working for him and he wants me to be lucky too."

"Come off it, surely neither of you believe that coloured glass can be lucky just because it's shaped like clover leaves?"

"He probably doesn't, but it was sweet of him to say that and find me a present I like. I do think they're lucky. Don't you remember what Rosie-Lee said about green being a lucky colour for me?"

"No." Stella sniffed her drink and stretched her mouth into a grimace.

"She did and you've got to admit she was right about everything else she saw for me. The number three obviously meant Trio and working with my senses was cooking and the job is perfect for me."

"The job is, but I'm not sure about the rest of it. You could say number four was luckier for you because it was Quattro opening that gave you the chance to be head chef."

"No, that was all down to Luigi. He's really done so much for me. He's taught me so much and made me much more confident and..."

"Yeah, yeah he's a great boss, I've got it. Be careful though, Daffs. I don't really trust him."

"Because he didn't fall apart when you dumped him?"

"No. It's not that. Not entirely. That blonde he was with when I went round there, he just snapped his fingers and expected her to come running, but he's not still seeing her you said. He uses people, Daffs. I don't want you to be next."

"Let's not fall out over him."

"No, let's not ever fall out over a bloke."

"Promise?"

"I promise."

They clinked glasses and each took a small sip. They poked their tongues out at each other.

"It tastes very green," Daphne said.

"Green and sweet."

"Talking of sweet, have you seen much of Doug?"

"Huh, fat lot of good he turned out to be."

"I thought you liked him?"

"I did, but he didn't feel the same way, obviously."

"He did, I heard him asking John for your number just a couple of days after the party. He said he must have written it down wrongly as the one you gave him didn't work. John teased him and said you'd probably given your old one just to get rid of him."

"Oh no! I bet I did."

"Make your mind up, do you want him to call or not?"

"I do. What I meant was that I hadn't had the phone long and after a couple of drinks, I probably gave out the wrong number by mistake. Did you tell him my new one?"

"John did."

"Great. He probably warned him off me as well."

Stella had been disappointed not to hear from Doug other than to receive a jokey Christmas card from him. Even that had been posted through Clover's letterbox rather than delivered in person. If John had warned him off then he'd have done so for a reason. Despite what she implied to Daphne, she knew he wasn't petty. Maybe unlike his sister,

John wasn't keen on Stella dating a tall, dark handsome man and had an alternative in mind.

Once Daphne had returned to work, Stella rang John to see if she could discover what he'd said to Doug and why.

"I didn't tell him anything, Stella. He's quite capable of making up his own mind. Daphne was another matter and kept on at him to ring you until the poor bloke was obliged to ask me for your number just to keep her quiet."

"Yeah, thanks, John."

"I'm sorry, I wouldn't normally give out your number to anyone, but it was obvious that Daphne would have told him if I didn't."

"When was this?"

"Last week."

"Doesn't sound as though he's as keen as Daphne seemed to think. I reckon she's still trying to fix me up with someone who fits what that stupid gypsy said."

"You could be right there."

"I don't think I should go along with what she says should happen, do you?"

"Your call," John said, completely missing his chance to agree that someone short and fair might suit her better than a tall, dark bloke.

"I mean, she can't know who or what I want after just talking to me for twenty minutes, can she?"

"Shouldn't think so, I haven't worked it out after twenty years."

"John, about that letter... Don't you think..."

"What letter?"

"The one the gypsy gave me and Daphne."

"You're not seeing that until the year's up, Stella," he said and immediately disconnected the call.

Stella kicked out in frustration, knocking Thirteen across the room. She rushed over to pick up the stuffed cat and stubbed her toe on the table leg.

"Argh!"

Sinking to the floor, she held the furry black toy in her arms and sobbed.

Stella couldn't face New Year's Eve on her own which meant she had to go to Trio. Even worse she wouldn't be eating and drinking; she'd be working! She could hardly believe she'd allowed Daphne to talk her into it.

"I don't have a clue about being a waitress," she'd pleaded.

"You're not going to be one really, you'll just be carrying stuff for the waiting staff we managed to persuade to work. Come on, you'll get paid and it'll help me out. Admit it, it's the best offer you've had."

It was.

Trio still looked elegant, even with extra tables crowded in. The tinkling piano music added to the classy atmosphere. If Stella hadn't seen the expensive music system she'd have expected to fall over a pianist en route to the kitchen. The restaurant smelled wonderful too; the aroma of rich sauces and fresh herbs filled the air.

Maybe as she'd made the floral decorations herself she was biased, but she thought they looked perfectly in keeping. She glowed with pride each time anyone said how pretty they were. Mr Clover had shown her the mechanics of preparing the flowers, creating the bases and cutting and wiring the stems so they were the right length to create a balanced display. It was Stella who'd picked out the flowers and foliage to use, selecting flower colours and shapes that worked well together. Knowing the light in Trio would be low and intimate, she'd chosen mostly white flowers highlighted with a few deepest red carnations to match the restaurant's decor. She'd used the faintest touch of silver spray on the grey-green eucalyptus leaves and sprigs of pine needles.

Stella spent the evening with an L plate on her pinny carrying stuff. Lots of stuff. It was incredibly hard work, but not difficult once she'd got used to the table numbering system. The few times she delivered food to the wrong table, the customers put her right with good-natured teasing. The teasing for the regular staff who made mistakes was louder, but still kindly meant.

After the first hour, she had to remove the T shirt she'd put on under the thin blouse, stick plasters on her ankles and swap her smart stilettos for a pair of soft pumps lent to her by Maria, the maitre d'. At least she wasn't alone watching TV in her drab flat and drinking a bottle of lurid green liqueur. She'd been given a lovely meal before the restaurant opened to customers and promised champagne at midnight.

Once customers began to order, she wasn't able to admire her surroundings. Immediately she was bringing platters of bread and olives, accompanied by tiny dishes of oil and vinegar, passata and pesto. No sooner had she set them down on one table than she'd be asked for jugs of iced water for another group. The time passed quickly. Soon she was summoned to collect a glass of champagne from Luigi and count down to the New Year. Everyone cheered, took a sip of their drink and kissed the person closest to them. Knowing that was likely, Stella had ensured she was nowhere near Luigi. Poor Daphne got lumbered with him.

As Stella turned to look for a suitable person to kiss, an arm circled her waist, pulling her towards its owner. She stiffened her body, holding it away from her captor as a pair of lips touched her own. After allowing him the briefest of kisses she pulled back her head to see who had hold of her.

It was John. "Happy New Year," he said and kissed her again.

Stella returned his kiss and allowed her body to relax into his embrace.

"I've got to get back to work, but couldn't resist the chance to start off the year as I'd very much like it to continue," John said.

Before Stella could reply, a waiter kissed her, then a waitress. Then the customers moved around, kissing each other and the staff. John had vanished, or maybe she'd imagined the whole thing. Stella was half asleep on her hot, tired feet by the time the last customer left Trio.

"Crikey, Daffs, I don't know how you cope with this every night. It's going to take me a week to recover."

"I'm tired too, but it isn't always as hectic as this. You get off home, there's not much more you can do here. We're just going to check everything's safe. You know, no burning candles or anything like that and then I'll be going home to bed too."

"You can crash at my place, if you'd rather not drive. Sorry, I should have thought to offer before," Stella said.

"Thanks. I will, it'll save me driving back in the morning."

"Go blow out your candles then, I'll wait here."

"Stella, time to go," Daphne said, shaking Stella.

"Er, what? Was I asleep?"

"Yes, come on sleeping beauty, let's get you home."

They were too tired to pull out the sofa bed and search for linen, so slept side by side in Stella's big bed with Thirteen laid across their feet. They were both asleep in minutes.

Stella awoke with a start, aware she wasn't alone. She turned to face the body next to hers. On the pillow was a head covered in fair hair. She leapt out of bed, pulled on her dressing gown and scurried out of her bedroom. In the bathroom the realisation she was wearing her pyjamas and that her feet ached helped her remember the night before. Once she'd washed, Stella made tea and carried a mug into Daphne.

"Morning. Oooh tea, thanks. What's the time?"

"Dunno, early." Stella yawned, got back into bed and pulled the quilt over her.

She'd forgotten how chirpy Daphne was from the moment she woke up. Hopefully Daphne would have remembered Stella needed time before she was capable of conversation.

"Early for you, or actually early?"

Stella made a heroic effort and pulled herself upright enough to gesture at her bedside clock.

Daphne kept quiet until they'd both drunk their tea and she'd been to the bathroom. "So, Stells, how come you're just about awake so early on your day off?" She said as she returned and perched on the bed.

"That's your fault. Didn't half give me a shock waking up to find a blonde in my bed. Did you know the top of your head looks exactly like your brother's?"

Daphne snorted with laughter. "That must have been a shock!"

"Not as much as you'd think." If she could imagine him appearing at Trio on the stroke of midnight to kiss her, then who knows where her tired brain might see him next?

"What?"

"Oh nothing."

"Come on, don't give me that. If you don't explain I'll be forced to assume you often accidentally wake up with John."

"Hmm. I don't think so." Stella whacked Daphne with a pillow.

"Ah, so it's deliberate?"

Stella whacked her again.

"You never get to sleep? Now I am shocked."

And again.

"No, maybe not." Daphne snatched the pillow from her friend and held it at arm's length. "What is it with you two? Why can't you be friends?"

"We are. I think."

"You were at Christmas, but that was last year. Things never stay the same with you two." She raised the pillow and dropped it onto Stella's head.

Stella tried to grab it back, but wasn't quick enough. "Nothing has changed since Christmas."

"Oh good. When he came into Trio last night and didn't talk to you, I thought you'd fallen out."

So, she hadn't been hallucinating. "He did, er, talk to me." Stella fiddled with her alarm, making sure it was set for the following morning.

"Good. Stells, is there something you're not telling me?"

"Of course not. We don't have secrets, do we?"

"No." Daphne didn't sound as convinced as Stella would have liked.

"It's just that I'm never quite sure about John. Sometimes he seems like he wants to be my friend and sometimes..."

"There's no sometimes about it. He deffo wants be your pal. Ignore anything else, it's just him being daft."

"Right. Good. Well... You've got two choices for breakfast. Either I scrape the furry bits off the bread and make toast or you make something interesting with the sad contents of my fridge."

Daphne said, "Or, option three, we go over to Trio and I make us a nice cheese and ham omelette and some decent coffee."

"Can you do that?"

"Yeah, didn't Rosie-Lee say three was my lucky number?"

"She did. You know me, I wouldn't want to argue with fate."

Daphne whacked her again with the pillow. "Don't even think of getting me back, or it's furry toast for you."

Stella dropped the second pillow and started dressing.

They'd eaten breakfast and were on their second cup of coffee when Luigi arrived. He greeted Daphne with an enthusiasm that bordered on sexual harassment and then tried to kiss Stella. The caffeine had sharpened up her reflexes and she managed an avoidance manoeuvre which limited the damage to a peck on the cheek.

"You forgot something yesterday, Stella," he said.

If he was referring to the leaning tower of washing up she was out of there. She needn't have worried, he produced an envelope.

"For helping out last night."

"Oh, thanks."

"Will you buy shoes?"

"Quite possibly." She managed a smile. He wasn't really such a bad bloke and the envelope felt quite thick.

"We have much to do today, Daphne will be busy."

And Stella was in the way. She could take a hint. "Right."

Once outside Trio, she looked inside the envelope. It contained far too much money for a few hours waitressing. Stella felt uncomfortable. Something wasn't right, but she didn't know what.

Chapter Thirteen

Stella returned to bed when she got home and slept for another two hours. After a shower she felt much better and decided it wasn't too late to make a New Year's resolution. The first one was to never get a job that involved rushing about in stilettos until nearly three in the morning. The second was to eat more chocolate. If she hadn't been sticking with last year's resolution, not to make resolutions she couldn't keep, she'd have made a third involving the words 'boy', 'get' and 'friend' although not in that order. As it was, she was quitting whilst she was ahead.

Her phone rang. It was John.

"Hi Stella, I'm really sorry, but I forget to mention Daphne's birthday to you. I hope you don't already have plans?"

"Daphne and I were going to go to the pictures."

"You wouldn't mind doing that another day, would you? Mum and Dad want to have a little surprise party for her. Obviously you're invited."

"Yeah, OK. What's the plan?"

"It's just a silly joke really. Apparently when we were out walking with Gran, they got talking about birthday parties and how they always did something unusual for Daphne, because they thought she might feel her special day was overshadowed by Christmas."

"Yeah, I remember. She had parties at Safari parks or ice rinks and there was the time it was a picnic on the beach."

"Not their best idea as I recall."

"So what are they doing this year?"

"Daphne said she'd been a deprived child because she'd never had the boring sort of birthday party other kids had. You know the sort of... Er, anyway they thought they'd do a kid's tea party with jelly and ice cream and play pass the parcel."

"Sounds great. What time will they want us? We were going to see the three-fifteen film."

"I'll speak to Mum and call you back."

In a valiant effort to keep her resolutions, Stella put on flat shoes and walked to the convenience store for chocolate. As they had a range of beauty product gift packs at a bargain price, she bought one. At home, she spent two hours exfoliating, moisturising and eating chocolate Flakes. This seemed like the perfect time to try out the nail polish, lipstick and blusher that various members of Daphne's family had given her for Christmas. Each item was pale pink and she wondered if that was coincidence. Probably, as they were different makes. They sort of matched a summer dress she had; Stella couldn't resist putting it on and completing the look with her fluffy slippers.

She studied herself in the mirror. From the ankles up she looked fabulous. Pity it was too cold to wear the dress out so nobody would see how gorgeous she looked. Never mind, she'd turn the heating up and see if she had any music that sounded tropical.

Stella's phone beeped. The text was from John.

'New Year resolution 2 B friends with U 2 stop my sister nagging. U in?'

Did he mean did she want to form a stop Daphne nagging pact, or was he asking if she was at home? She wasn't sure it was possible to be friends with someone when every communication resulted in misunderstanding. It was worth a try though.

'Yes,' she texted back.

Her intercom buzzed.

"It's your friend John here, can I come up?"

Stella pressed the door release and took a couple of deep breaths.

"Hey, you look great," he said when she let him in.

"I'm in denial."

"Oh. I'm sorry..." He looked as though she'd just announced she had a week to live.

"Hey, what's up? I know we haven't always got on, but even I don't blame you for the weather."

"Weather?"

"Yes. I'm pretending it's summer."

"Oh. Good."

What was up with him? "What's up with you?"

"I thought I might have upset you earlier, talking about birthday parties."

"No. I got jelly and ice cream and played pass the parcel lots of times. It's fine, honestly. I just hope Daphne isn't disappointed. She hasn't missed out on much."

"Right. Good. Mum said she thought it would be good if you could pretend you're still going to the cinema and for me to meet you there and drive us all over at about three thirty. How's that sound?"

"Great." It also sounded like something he could have told her over the phone, so there must be more.

"Cup of tea?" she offered.

"That'd be great."

Waiting for the kettle to boil, she realised what the something more was. He'd thought he'd upset her and had come to check she was OK. John was actually a nice bloke who'd had the decency to turn up just when she was looking fab and feeling extremely bored.

She made the tea, handed him a mug and carried hers into the living room. He followed and sat next to her on the sofa.

"I'd offer you something to eat, but even Daffs couldn't make a meal out of what's in my fridge."

"Good grief, it must be bad."

"Not really, I've got chocolate." She indicated the flakes and hoped that if he noticed there were only two left in the pack, he wouldn't guess she'd bought it that morning.

"You'd share your chocolate with me? I'm flattered."

"Well, I'm just that nice." She grinned and fluttered her eyelashes.

"You have your moments."

"Oi cheeky, just for that I'm going to make you play Trivial Pursuit."

"Noooo."

"Yes, unless you've got to go to work."

"No, unfortunately not. Er, yes. Yes, I do. I mean I'm sure I can hear a kitten up a tree mewing for me to rescue it."

"It's firemen who do that." Stella went to the cupboard her television sat on.

"It is? So that's where I've been going wrong all these years."

She put the Trivial Pursuit box on the coffee table and pulled off the lid.

"What colour do you want to be?" Stella asked as she set up the board.

John gave an exaggerated sigh. "Blue, of course, and you needn't think I'm going to help you."

John was pretty good at answering his questions. Even 'What TV spy organisation fought the Technological Hierarchy for the Removal of Undesirables and Subjugation of Humanity?' didn't stump him.

"Uncle," he said whilst she was still trying to pronounce subjugation.

"Your uncle presumably as I don't have any relations."

"No, U.N.C.L.E. As in *The Man from Uncle*."

"Ah, OK." Something told her she might not win this one.

Fortunately, he was even better at giving clues when she couldn't answer hers. The game was fairly even by the time John told her he really did have to go.

"I'll see you on the third then," she said as he lingered in her doorway.

"Yes. Looking forward to it." He still didn't go. "Thanks for the tea and the game and everything."

"You're welcome."

"You look great, did I mention that?"

"You did, but I'll forgive you for repeating yourself."

"Will you forgive this?" He leant forward and gave her a quick kiss.

It wasn't the same as the Christmas Day kiss, or even the New Year one, but it was the best one she'd had all year. Friendly, that's what it was.

"I forgive you. Now go arrest the bad guys."

"I didn't plan this," Daphne said when she spotted John outside the cinema.

"I know you didn't," Stella agreed.

"You do?"

"Absolutely. I didn't plan it either, but I went along with it."

"With what?"

"It's a surprise, Sis, come on," John said.

On the drive he explained about the party. That didn't prepare Daphne for the sight of their parents' house decorated with balloons and banners and guests dressed in school uniform. She squealed with excitement as Stella and John disappeared to change.

Several staff from Trio had been invited and were introduced as 'Stella's dear little friends from school'. Even Luigi got into the spirit of the thing and had dressed up, although he said he was the headmaster and opted for a mortar board and cloak instead of the short trousers and blazer John was wearing. The shorts showed off his muscular legs and the unbuttoned shirt gave a glimpse of his hairy chest, so he looked both cute and naughty as well as strong and dependable. Stella didn't know who'd supplied the outfit she was wearing, but they'd obviously thought she was on the small side. The effect was slightly St Trinian's; thank goodness she'd shaved her legs recently.

As well as the promised jelly and ice cream, they all ate hotdogs and crisps and drank cherryade. They played statues, pass the parcel and musical chairs. Sadly nobody suggested spin the bottle or sardines, but the goody bags partly made up for that. Stella's contained a candy necklace, colouring book and hair slides decorated with shiny fairies.

"Stella," John called as she was on her way to get changed.

He must be in a hurry to take her home. "I won't be long." She ran up the stairs.

"Hang on a minute." He followed her.

"What's up?"

"Nothing, I just thought that, um... Would you like to go out sometime?"

"Oh!" Daphne must have had a word with him. "As friends do you mean?"

He started to answer, but was drowned out by Daphne calling her. "Stells, come and get changed, John's got to get to work this evening."

"Have you?"

He nodded.

"I'll be right back." She raced up a couple more steps, then stopped and turned. "Yes," she said, to John's retreating back. He didn't seem to have heard her. Never mind, there would be plenty more chances for her to say yes.

Sunday was a quiet day. At eleven in the evening, she discovered that was partly explained by her phone being completely flat. There were four missed calls, one from Daphne and three from John. There was also a text message from John saying she'd left her goody bag in his car and he'd drop it round when he had a chance and asking her to call him if she was free Sunday afternoon.

One Monday, as Stella passed Trio on her way to work, she saw Luigi open the door to his flat and look left and right like a spy in a dodgy film. She couldn't tell if he'd spotted her and considered ignoring him. That'd be childish she reasoned so put up a hand to acknowledge him. He leapt back inside only to emerge a moment later and wave back. Later that day he came into the florist's and ordered an extravagant bouquet.

"It is for a friend who works very hard."

Clearly something was going on. He'd never explained his floral purchases when they'd been going out together and since she'd seen the blonde in his flat it was too late to worry about making her jealous. Come to think of it, he'd been acting oddly even before he'd noticed her, so whatever he was up to wasn't directly related to her. She was going to have to keep an eye on him.

Stella took a longer route to and from the florist so she could watch the back entrance of Trio before and after work and walked past the restaurant during her lunch breaks to observe the front. One morning she saw a local deli's van at the back of Trio. The men moved fast, carrying wrapped trays. She'd heard a local shop now sold pizza and Daphne had said the restaurant was far too busy for her to keep up with all the cooking so Luigi had arranged extra help. She should have paid more attention, not switched off when his name was mentioned. He must be passing off shop bought stuff as his own authentic cuisine. That was a cheat! Was it even legal?

John walked into the shop just after eleven. He made a few random comments, mostly about the weather, each time she was without a customer. He said her hair looked nice and thanked her twice for the musical socks she'd given him for Christmas.

"Is there something you want to say?" she asked eventually.

"Two things, but it's a bit awkward. Daphne wouldn't want me to say anything..."

Maybe he'd noticed Luigi acting suspiciously too.

"Is this about Luigi?"

"Yes." He looked even more uncomfortable.

Of course Daphne would want to be loyal to her boss and that made things awkward for John.

"Maybe this isn't the best place to discuss it?" she said.

"You're right. Can I meet you for a coffee in your lunch break. We can talk properly then."

Good, at least he was taking the matter seriously.

She put on lippy and a spritz of perfume. It wasn't all for John's benefit, she wanted to be sure he didn't tell Daphne she was pining away for Luigi and give her another excuse to fix her up with someone. Especially if that someone was another friend of John's who'd turn up late, flirt like crazy so she looked like a two timing tart and then lose interest.

Stella was pleased to see John was waiting for her in the coffee shop and had already bought her a cappuccino. "So, what are you going to do about Luigi?" she demanded.

"Do about him?"

"Yes. You are going to look into this?"

"Um, yes. Er, perhaps you'd better tell me exactly what you think is going on."

Stella gave a detailed account of what she'd seen. It didn't sound so convincing when she said it out loud.

"Don't worry, Mozzarella, I dough think there's anything to worry about, so that should give you pizza mind."

"Don't you dare laugh at me!"

"I'm not. I'm just trying to be friendly."

"You've got a strange way of doing that; hardly speaking one minute, sneaking into Trio and kissing me the next."

"I was not sneaking. It was New Year's Eve, I was working in the area, so went to say Happy New Year to my sister."

"Your sister?"

"Yes. It was New Year and people do kiss each other at New Year."

"Yes."

"And at Christmas."

"Yes, well I'd better get back to work." Stella crashed painfully into another table as she fled the coffee shop. He'd said there were two things he wanted to say, but she'd already heard more than enough. Obviously he'd only made his clumsy attempts at friendship because Daphne had nagged him, had he been going to say Luigi had dated her for the same reason?

Stella broke two vases at work before Mr Clover suggested she clear out one of the store rooms. The hard work involved helped a bit, but she was still angry. Angry at herself for thinking John's kisses had meant anything and angry with him for laughing at her. That night, she lay awake wondering how many people failed to report crimes because of the unsympathetic police reaction.

She woke with her heart pounding and the quilt wrapped tightly around her. Had she really heard a noise from the unoccupied flat below, or was that part of the nightmare? For the first time, having the whole building to herself didn't seem such an advantage. Her instinct was to take a look and reassure herself she really was alone, but remembering the recent burglaries in the area, decided that was unwise. She stayed where she was and listened.

Stella heard the sound of footsteps. In the silence it seemed just as though someone were in her flat. He was here! The man John had warned her about was in her flat. Holding her breath she waited. There was another noise, like something being dragged over the ground or a floor. Not in the flat though. Outside, or below her in the building? For what seemed a long time she lay perfectly still listening to her own breathing and the distant rumble of traffic. Eventually she decided she was alone in the flat but it was still possible someone else was in the building.

Calling the police would be sensible, but John was probably on night shift and she wouldn't give him the satisfaction of laughing at her for being scared of something going bump in the night. The door to her flat was locked; wasn't it? She couldn't remember. There was a heavy torch and her mobile by the bed; she was safe and should go back to sleep. Or try to.

A glance at the clock showed her it wasn't as late as she'd thought and Trio would only just have closed. Daphne might have seen something as she drove by on her way home and she wouldn't be asleep yet. Stella rang her mobile.

Daphne said, "Actually, I haven't been by yet. We were, I was... I'll come round now and make sure you're OK."

Stella waited, listening out for further sounds. Every creak of the old building made her jump. Other than passing cars, there was nothing to suggest there was anyone but her awake in the whole street until she heard a door opening. Stella held her breath until Daphne called out.

"Hi Stella, everything looks OK down here, I'm coming up."

Stella heard the sound again; she hadn't imagined it. This time she could also hear Daphne closing the street door and her footsteps echoing in the corridor.

A woman screamed and Stella heard the sound of someone running.

"Daphne?" Stella inched her door open and switched on the landing light. She crept forward and peered over the banister. A body lay at the bottom of the stairs.

Grabbing her phone, she ran down to Daphne. Stella sank onto the bottom step and punched 999 into her mobile.

"She's unconscious and bleeding from her head. Her leg's all twisted, it must be broken. Please hurry."

She held Daphne's limp hand and whispered, "Help's coming, just hold on."

Chapter Fourteen

As Stella chewed her nails in the hospital corridor the words, 'Please be OK, Daphne, please be OK,' pounded through her head. Each time anyone in uniform appeared she held her breath until they walked past. That they didn't stop to give her bad news was the best she could hope for. Daphne had been so pale and fragile looking as they stretchered her into the ambulance and so deeply unconscious during the journey to hospital that it was too early to hope she was now recovered.

Daphne's skin had been the colour of undercooked egg white, sharply contrasted against the dark red of her blood. Stella needed to look at something to take away that image. She picked up a glossy magazine and turned the pages. Words and images made no impression until she came to the horoscopes. The magazine was last month's, so wouldn't contain a warning for Daphne to avoid burglars on dimly lit stairs. Stella read through the dated forecasts for herself and Daphne. They seemed like the usual generalised platitudes and didn't mention anything that matched real events from last December. Rosie-Lee's predictions had been better. At least they'd been tailored to Stella and Daphne rather than a twelfth of the population. The gypsy had made a few specific claims too, one of them that Stella would save Daphne's life. It was Stella who'd made the call that caused Daphne to be pushed downstairs, so she felt more guilty than heroic. She had called the ambulance though, that had to count for something. Maybe that's what the gypsy had meant? If there was any truth in her words, then Daphne would recover. For the first time ever, Stella longed to be able to tell Daphne how accurate the prediction had been.

She didn't notice John arrive until he was standing in front of her. Stella stumbled towards him. He wrapped his arms around her and held her tight.

"Oh, John, I'm so sorry," she sobbed against his shoulder.

"Have you heard anything new?" he asked.

"They wouldn't tell me much; just that they're doing all they can," she told him.

"I'm sure that's true." He stroked her hair until she stopped crying. "Will you be OK while I go and ask?"

Stella nodded. She knew he'd get answers: a policeman who was the patient's brother wouldn't be fobbed off with bland reassurances.

"Please be OK, Daphne," she whispered again as she sat on the orange plastic chair and hugged her arms around her knees. The ambulance had arrived quickly and Daphne went straight to casualty; speed helped, didn't it? Why had she called Daphne, instead of just going back to sleep and ignoring the sounds she'd heard?

John returned and put a hand on her shoulder. "She's going to be OK," he said.

"Really?"

"Yes. It looked worse than it was, Stella. She's lost a lot of blood but they've stopped the bleeding now and set her broken leg. It'll take her a while to recover, but she'll be fine."

"You're sure?"

"I saw her. She's sleeping, her leg is covered by bandages and a box thing, but she looks OK. Peaceful, a reasonable colour and not hooked up to dozens of machines. I've phoned Mum and Dad, they're on the way."

"It was all my fault."

"No," said John. "It wasn't. Someone is to blame, but it isn't you. I'll need a statement, Stella."

His sharp tone did more to calm her than sympathy would have done.

"Now?"

"If you feel up to it. It would be best to make a note of the facts now. A female officer will take your statement and if you want a counsellor I can arrange that. This must have been a terrible shock for you. Sorry, I was just thinking of Daphne."

"I'd like to do all I can to catch whoever did this."

John nodded and then used his radio to tell his colleague that Stella was ready to give a statement.

John removed the magazine from the chair next to Stella's and sat down. Neither of them spoke until a policewoman arrived a few minutes later and introduced herself to Stella.

"I'll leave you to it, then," he said.

"No. Please, could you stay?"

"Sure."

It helped to have him close, but not need to look at him. Stella gave him an account of the evening's events. Whenever she thought she was about to cry, he squeezed her hand.

Gently, the policewoman questioned Stella.

"Could you describe the man? Even a small detail might help."

"I didn't see him, but I'm sure he was in my flat and..."

"And what?" the officer prompted.

"It's stupid... " Stella turned to John. "You're not going to laugh, right?"

She looked at his face: he wouldn't laugh.

"I dreamed a tall, dark, handsome, heavy-breathing stranger was admiring me and took my picture."

"Heavy breathing?" the policewoman asked.

"Yes. I wasn't scared of that in the dream, but remembering it now, it seems horrible." Stella shuddered.

John squeezed her hand. "We'll catch him, whoever it was."

When Stella had given every detail she could remember, the policewoman read through her notes to check they were correct.

"I'll get these typed up before you sign them. If you remember anything else let one of us know and I'll add it in." The policewoman shook Stella's hand and left.

"Thanks for being kind, John," Stella said.

"Despite what you think about me, I don't torture witnesses."

"No, but you might have blamed me for putting your sister in danger."

"Actually, I blame myself. If we got along better you might have called me instead of Daphne."

"Look, we could blame ourselves all night. You were right, we didn't hurt her, the burglar did. What's important now is that you catch him and we both help her recover."

"When she comes round from the op you can reassure her you're OK and I'll promise to catch the bad guy," John said. "Then if you could help me to get clothes and stuff for her I'd appreciate it. Mum would just fuss and bring a wardrobe full just in case and you'd know better than me what to bring."

"That's fine. I'll go to the restaurant and let them know. Daphne won't want people worrying about her."

"Do you want me to see Luigi? It might be awkward for you..."

"It'll be OK. Daphne keeps telling me what a great boss he is and I think me and him are more than quits since my performance at his party." Stella didn't meet John's eyes.

"Hmm, so you're completely over him?"

"Totally."

"Stella, about Luigi and Daphne..."

"What? You don't think it was him do you, who pushed her? Maybe she found out what he's up to buying in pizzas, or he knew I'd found out and he was trying to silence us. Is it something to do with the Mafia?"

"Calm down. Luigi is buying in cheese and pepperoni and selling pre-prepared pizza to the deli. Sorry to break it to you, Stella, but an Italian restaurant owner selling pizza is business, not a crime, even if he did cheat on you."

"He did not cheat on me; I dumped him! That girl was just someone he contacted to save face in front of his mum; he's not interested... and like I said, I'm not bothered. So he was just buying ingredients and selling pizzas?"

"Yep."

"Oh."

Could she have misunderstood what she'd seen? Yes, probably as she'd only got a quick look. The polythene wraps must have just been to protect the food, not to disguise the evidence. That made more sense than him buying in pizzas. Stella had wondered how he'd have been able to do that without Daphne knowing about it.

"So why did he act so suspiciously?"

"Perhaps he didn't like you snooping about?"

"I wasn't." That didn't sound convincing, even to herself. She had been snooping on Luigi and expecting to discover something that would show him in a bad light. It was almost inevitable that she'd have eventually seen something unusual and jumped to the wrong conclusion. Why was she always such a rotten judge of people?

She yawned.

"I'll go and see what's happening," John said and again left her waiting in the hospital corridor.

He wasn't gone long.

"Mum and Dad have just arrived and are going to stay with Daphne. She's stable and sleeping peacefully. It's late, I suggest we do the same."

Stella nodded.

"Come on then." He held out a hand to help her up.

"Sorry, yes." Stella walked down the corridor without releasing his hand. She shivered.

"Here, it's been a horrible night for you," John said. He draped his jacket round her shoulders. "Let's get you home."

He put the heating on full for the short drive home, but she couldn't stop shivering.

Ignoring the double yellow lines, John pulled up right outside the street entrance to her flat. There was stripy tape tied in a zig-zag between the gutter down-pipe on one side and the estate agent's board on the other. More was wrapped around the knocker and caught up in the letter box.

"Damn," John said. "I'd forgotten about that."

"What is that? It looks like a crime scene off TV."

"It is a crime scene. Sorry, Stella but you can't go in."

"But... how long for?"

"Shouldn't be long. I expect you'll be able to get back in tomorrow, but if not, I'll make arrangements for you to go in and get some of your things."

"Where will I sleep tonight?"

"My place."

"Your place? I've heard of some strange things men do to persuade girls to spend the night with them, but having her flat covered with police tape is a first." Stella started to laugh. She didn't know why as she wasn't finding this funny, but she couldn't stop herself.

"Stella, stop it!" John said as he gripped her shoulders. "You're tired and upset and in danger of getting hysterical."

"Sorry," she muttered as she calmed down.

"Stella, look at me."

She did.

"I didn't plan this. I should have realised earlier that you probably wouldn't be able to go home tonight. I'm sorry I forgot, but I was worried about Daphne."

She nodded. Now she thought about it, it didn't seem so odd that the police would need to come back in daylight to check for clues and take photographs. Neither did it seem strange that John's concern for his sister had meant he hadn't considered that.

"You can stay in Daphne's bed, we both know she wouldn't mind."

Stella nodded again.

"So you're not really staying at my place, you're staying at Daphne's. This is not some elaborate plot to get you to spend the night with me."

"No, of course not. I'm sorry I..."

"You're my sister's friend so I'm concerned for you and you're too tired to find anywhere else to sleep, that's all it is. I'm not making a move on you."

"OK, I understand."

"I don't particularly want you hanging about tomorrow as I've got a lot to do, but I don't want you contaminating any evidence so I've got to put up with it."

"OK, John, I get it. Can we go now please?"

They didn't speak again until they were inside the flat John shared with his sister.

"Tea?" he offered.

"Please."

She was very tired, but didn't think she'd sleep and wanted his company. Even talking to John would be better than being left alone with her thoughts. She curled up on the sofa.

"There you go," he said handing her a steaming mug and sitting next to her. "That's two you owe me now."

She remembered the time he'd come round for tea and they'd been so busy talking she'd forgotten to make it. They could be nice to each other if they tried and now, when they were both worried about Daphne, was a good time to try.

"Seems you'll have to wait until the police have done their investigations. I could buy some chocolate Hobnobs, would you accept one as interest?"

"Make it two and you have a deal." He briefly squeezed her shoulder.

They didn't talk as they sipped their tea, but she was glad she was with him. Gradually she warmed up and began to feel safer. She was dozing when he kissed her cheek and said it was time for bed.

"Night, John."

Stella peeled off her clothes, dropped them by the side of Daphne's bed and crawled under the quilt. Daphne had been taken to the hospital very quickly and already had the operation to put right her injuries. She'd be OK. She had to be OK.

It was barely light when Stella awoke. She reached out for the alarm to check if she'd remembered to set it yesterday and wondered if it was worth trying to get back to sleep for a while. Stella had to stare at the strange clock for quite a while before she realised where she was and that it was lunchtime. She dropped Daphne's clock, rolled over in bed and grabbed her phone.

"Mr Clover, it's Stella. I'm so sorry, I've just woken up. My friend was taken to hospital yesterday after she had a fall at my flat. She was knocked out and broke her leg. I didn't get to bed until... well, I don't know what time it was."

"It's all right," her boss assured her. "Your friend's brother came round and explained. I'm sure you'll want a couple of days off to recover from the shock and to be with poor Daphne."

Whatever had John said?

"Thanks, I'll see you Saturday then," she said before Mr Clover could change his mind.

Even the brief details she'd given Mr Clover reminded Stella of how Daphne had looked lying in a pool of blood at the bottom of her stairs. There was no hope of getting back to sleep now, so she dragged herself out of bed, pulled on Daphne's dressing gown and went into the kitchen.

Stella found a note by the kettle. 'I knew you'd be tired, so I've explained to your boss that you were at the hospital all night. Hope that was OK? Speak to you later. J x'

John came back just as the kettle boiled. "OK?" he asked.

"Yes. I didn't think I'd sleep, but I've only just got up. I was just making a cup of tea, do you want one?"

"Great, thanks."

"Any news about Daphne?"

"She's doing OK, I hear. Mum and Dad booked into the Travel Lodge and took it in turns to stay with her all night. As she's still a bit sleepy from the anaesthetic, I haven't been in to see her yet. I did call into the station though. Your statement has been typed up ready for you to sign."

"You must be exhausted."

"No, I'm fine. I'm used to working shifts. You'll be pleased to hear you can now get back in your place. I'll take you home whenever you're ready."

"Thanks, John."

They went via the police station. Stella read through her statement. Although she knew it was all true, the slightly official sounding language used made it seem like something that had happened to someone else. She signed the forms in the places indicated.

Instead of dropping her off in the street outside her flat and rushing home to get some sleep, John again parked on the double yellow lines. He removed the police tape and went inside the building with her. Stella gasped when she saw the blood-covered hallway.

Chapter Fifteen

It was only John's arm tight around her waist which stopped Stella sinking down onto the bloody floor.

"We'd better clear this up," John said as calmly as though someone had spilt a pint of milk. "Could you get a bowl of warm water, a bin bag and old cloths or something?"

She rushed away from the gruesome sight. Upstairs, Stella filled the small bucket she used for mopping her kitchen floor, added lemon scented cleaner, grabbed a pack of kitchen cloths and tore a bin bag from the roll. When Stella returned, she saw John had wiped up the worst of the blood with newspapers from her recycling bin. He stuffed the papers into the bin bag and helped Stella mop up the rest of the mess. The soiled cloths were added to the bin bag before John tied it tightly.

"I'll get rid of this for you."

He left the bag in the hallway and carried the bucket back to her flat.

"Are you ready for another cup of tea?" she asked.

"More tea? You're obsessed with the stuff! Yeah, go on then, just a quick one. I'm going to get a couple hours sleep, then look in on Daphne. Would you like me to come round afterwards and let you know how she's doing?"

"Yes, thanks. Give her my love, will you?"

"Of course." John gulped down his tea. "Thanks for this. You still owe me one though, don't forget."

"And a chocolate Hobnob."

"Two. I'm not letting you get away with that."

She grinned at him. It was much better when they were friends.

It seemed John thought so too because he gave her a quick hug before he left and said, "Try not to worry, I'll call you if there's any definite news and I'll be back soon."

Stella had a shower and made herself more tea in a fresh mug; the one she'd used earlier had vanished. After drinking it, she decided to put on some make-up. It would be bad enough for John to see his sister looking rough, he didn't need the sight of Stella in the same state. A touch of blusher helped but her eyes still looked tired. She dabbed illuminating cream over the shadows underneath. That didn't help at all, so she removed it and reached for the mascara.

How long had she been in the shower? She checked her phone but she hadn't missed a call. Of course not; John said he'd come back and let her know how Daphne was doing. People usually gave bad news in person. No, there wasn't any bad news. If Daphne were in danger, he'd have been in to see her earlier and John wouldn't lie to her. Getting worked up wouldn't help Daphne. She needed to stay calm. She'd do her nails, that usually soothed her.

The sight of her ragged chewed nails did help distract her attention and the action of filing and then painting them at least stopped her jumping up to check her phone or chew them down any shorter.

That illuminating cream might be OK if she blended it in properly. In the bathroom she found the missing mug. She returned it to the kitchen and put it in the sink next to John's.

A glance in the mirror showed only one set of lashes was coated with mascara. She put that right, added a slick of lipstick and decided to quit whilst she was ahead. Overall she managed to give the impression of someone who might have spent the night at hospital desperately worried, but managed to get some sleep and although they had no idea what to do with lipstick and blusher, had at least tried.

Reading was out of the question, she learnt after scanning the same line four times. There wasn't likely to be anything interesting on the television and listening to music didn't appeal. She had to do something, look at something to block out the thought of Daphne lying at the bottom of the stairs. She dragged out her photo album and flicked through it. There was a picture of Daphne being pushed on a swing by John. Just after Stella had taken it, Daphne had tried posing for a more dramatic shot by standing up and gone flying through the air with such speed the camera had caught nothing but a blur. Stella and John had run towards Daphne, who lay still and silent on the hard grass surround. They'd thought she was dead, but she'd just been winded. Her recovery from her latest incident might not be so instantaneous, but Daphne was tough, she would recover.

John arrived at half past four. "I forgot your bag from the party, sorry."

"What? Oh, it doesn't matter about that. Come and sit down and tell me how Daphne is."

"They've had to put pins in her leg. The doctor said the operation was successful, but she needs to rest and he's given her a sedative, so she'll be asleep for most of the day. She was just about awake when I saw her, but not feeling too good after the anaesthetic. You remember what she was like when she had her tonsils out?"

Stella did; Daphne had been sick on her when she'd visited. "Yes, do you remember this?" She handed him the swing photo.

"I do. We thought she was dead, didn't we?"

"She didn't speak for over a minute, so who could blame us?"

"What about that time with the giraffes?" John asked. He tugged at his own hair, presumably to remind her of the animal's tongue slobbering over Daphne's plaits.

"She talked then all right."

"I wouldn't call that noise talking."

It felt right to laugh with him. How strange that having so many shared memories didn't make her and John feel closer. There was never a time she'd felt any of the sisterly feelings for him that she and Daphne shared.

John's stomach rumbled.

"Haven't you eaten?" Stella asked.

"No. Have you?"

"No. That's not going to help anyone. Fancy scrambled egg on buttered toast and a mug of tea?"

"You're a wonderful woman, Stella."

"True." She grinned at him. "What you were saying the other day about us being friends. I'd like that."

He nodded.

"I'll make lunch or supper or whatever it is. Afraid you're going to have to wait for the biscuit though, I'm out of them."

She found she'd left the milk on the worktop. Careful concentration ensured she didn't season the eggs with sugar or try to toast her chopping board.

John was dozing on the sofa when she came in to lay the table. She watched him for a while, wondering if she should put a blanket around him and let him sleep. He might have to go to work though, so after putting their meal ready, she gently shook him. He opened his eyes, smiled at her and pulled her down for a hug.

"Oh, Stella."

"Steady on, it's just scrambled eggs," she said laughing to show she wasn't annoyed and to cover the fact that her impulse had been to snuggle up next to him and let the food go cold. That probably wasn't the sort of thing he did with his friends though.

They ate without speaking. When they'd finished eating, he washed the plates and she dried them. They returned to the sofa where he explained about visiting Daphne.

"The doctor said I could go back about six and hopefully she'll be more alert by then. I'm not sure if it'll be family only. They didn't say."

"Maybe I'll go and see Luigi before I visit her then. Have you spoken to him?"

"I just left a message to say she couldn't come to work. I'm on duty and if I'd arrived in uniform to announce she was in hospital..."

"Yeah, we don't want to upset poor Luigi, do we?"

"Stella, I did say I'd speak to him if you prefer."

"No, sorry. It's fine, really. It's just that I'm fed up with hearing how great he is and how sensitive."

"I suppose Daphne is a bit biased in his favour, but she would be."

"Yeah, we've been through that. He's a great boss so she loves him, but a rotten boyfriend so I don't."

"So you're not over him?"

"I am, totally. Don't go thinking I'm jealous of how well they get on."

"Good. I assume you'd like to see Daphne today?"

"Of course, if they'll let me."

"They will if she's up to it, I expect, as she'll want to see you. I'll pick you up at six, if that's OK and we can pack stuff for her before we go in. Be gentle with poor Luigi, he's not as heartless as you think."

She didn't remember ever saying Luigi was heartless. There was no doubt that he liked Daphne and would be upset to hear she was injured, not just inconvenienced because one of his key members of staff would be out of action for a while. He already knew she wasn't coming to work that day so it wasn't as though he'd be worrying about her, so there was no need for her to rush round there. On the other hand, if she put it off she'd just become even more reluctant.

A glance at the clock showed the lunchtime session at Trio would be over and they'd just be ready to dispose of any uneaten desserts. That thought meant Stella felt strong enough to walk to Trio. As she reached the bottom of the stairs and saw the spotlessly clean floor, she promised herself she'd try to be nicer to John in future. He must have been just as worried and just as tired as her when he'd ensured Stella didn't have to walk through his sister's blood.

Stella wasn't entirely sure whether it was worry about Daphne or just the icy wind that brought tears to her eyes. Trudging down the High Street felt as hard physically as it was mentally. She'd much rather be warm at home than have to battle against the weather and then against the awful memories of last night to explain what had happened to Daphne. Even the door to the restaurant seemed to be putting up a fight.

"Stella?" Luigi rushed to her as she burst into Trio. "Daphne, is she very ill?"

"She's had an accident and is in hospital, Luigi. They operated last night."

He sagged as though she'd punched him in the stomach. Stella led him to his office and pushed him into a chair. Explaining Daphne's injuries in as calm and reassuring manner as possible helped reassure her too. "John said she will be allowed visitors this evening, so I'm going with him."

"May I see her?" He looked pitiful.

"I don't know, Luigi. I'll ask when I'm there and let you know."

"If only I had come with her last night. I wouldn't have allowed her to go if I'd known what would happen."

He was rather overdoing the emotional Latin hero in Stella's opinion. Was he really so conceited he thought this was anything to do with him?

"I wouldn't have wanted her to come if I'd really thought there was someone there, but we couldn't have stopped her," Stella pointed out as reasonably as she could. If Luigi wanted to blame himself that was his problem, she wasn't going to add to the guilt she already felt.

"No. She would always want to save you from any hurt. That is why..."

"What?"

"She wanted to tell you herself, but she couldn't bear to hurt you."

"Tell me what?" Did the man have to make a drama out of everything?

"Daphne and I, we are... I love her."

It felt as though the filthy weather had burst into the restaurant and then suddenly blown itself out so they were now in a dead calm; or was this the eye of the storm?

Chapter Sixteen

"I love Daphne," Luigi repeated.

"Oh." Now it was Stella who needed the support of a chair. After a couple of gulps for air she felt much better. Is that what it had been like for Daphne when she'd come off the swing? A few seconds of not being able to breathe followed by the realisation that she was fine. If Luigi was compared to a swing, then it was one she'd long since tired of. He never had pushed her up to an emotional high; that's probably why she'd never had to crash back down to earth.

Luigi was trying to explain. "I don't think she feels the same way, not yet. She is attracted, I know, but she won't come out with me before she has your blessing."

It made sense. Stella had been so sure Daphne was falling in love, but couldn't understand why she wouldn't discuss her mystery man. They'd shared almost everything over the years. The only time Stella had kept anything from Daphne had been when she'd been dating John; it hadn't seemed right to go into too much detail with his sister. No actually that wasn't entirely true. Stella hadn't shared many details of her relationship with Luigi either; Daphne hadn't seemed to want to know.

Daphne probably didn't like to tell Stella she was attracted to her ex. As soon as she saw Daphne, Stella would show her it was all right. First though, she'd need to convince herself it was all right. Luigi did seem sincere in his feelings for Daphne and in any case, love was an ideal incentive for Daffers to get herself up out of her hospital bed and into... well, to be with Luigi.

Luigi and Daphne would be perfect together, but she wasn't about to tell him that. He thought his charm meant he could get away with anything. It usually did, but he needn't think he could use Daphne in the same way he'd used the blonde he'd enticed into his flat after Stella had dumped him.

"I'm happy to give Daphne my blessing as you call it, but I'm not so sure about you. You'd better not hurt her. I'll be keeping an eye on you."

"You will be good at that. You caught me red-handed before with... Stella I am so sorry about that. If I'd imagined you'd come with me, I'd never have invited Rebecca. She is a girl I knew before and have remained friends with. I had booked flights and hotel rooms for two people..." He shrugged as if he thought a full explanation wasn't necessary.

"Oh and you used both rooms did you?" She knew this wasn't the time to settle old scores, but couldn't help the sarcastic tone.

"Yes, of course. Rebecca is not my lover."

He did seem very sure about that. Seems she'd misjudged him again.

"Well what's done is done but don't ever let me catch you with another woman when you're dating my friend."

Luigi smiled. "You almost caught Daphne coming out of my flat one day after I'd persuaded her to come back with me for a nightcap. Knowing she wouldn't want you to see her, I pushed her back inside and waved at you, but I'm sure you thought I was up to something."

"I did."

"I wasn't; not really. I carried her to my bed when she fell asleep and I slept on the sofa. There was nothing... "

"I believe you." Poor Luigi, it seemed all his romantic attempts resulted in him falling asleep on the sofa.

"Daphne said she would like to be my friend and to spend time with me, but it couldn't be more until she was very sure that you'd not be hurt."

"I won't be. If she can be happy with you then I'll be happy for you."

"So you trust me?"

She daren't tell him that, until recently, she couldn't decide if he was part of the Mafia or simply involved in culinary fraud, but maybe the time would come when she, Daphne and Luigi could laugh about that together.

"I'll tell Daphne it's OK with me if she goes out with you, but I'm not going to try to talk her into anything."

"Thank you, Stella."

The wind was at her back for the walk home. It seemed to be supporting her as it gently pushed her home.

Daphne's parents were still at her bedside when Stella and John arrived at the hospital. They hugged John, then Stella, just as though she was one of the family.

"We'll leave you two with her for a while and go and get something to eat," Daphne's dad said.

"We'll be back later," her mum assured Daphne.

"The nurses don't seem to want us hanging around now, which is a good sign," Daphne's dad said. "If she was in danger they'd want us here. As it is, they keep hinting that she needs to rest."

"Go and eat," John said. "We'll stay with Daphne as long as she wants us here and go if she wants to sleep." As he finished speaking, he turned his mum away from the bed and gave her a gentle push.

Daphne looked so vulnerable on the hospital bed. Stella was grateful to John for squeezing her hand and pointing out Daphne wasn't holding a bowl so hopefully no longer felt sick.

"I'm going to be fine," Daphne said in reply to their queries. She looked through the bag of loose, comfortable clothes John handed her. "Thanks, Stella."

"How do you know I didn't pack those?" John asked.

"The bag you dropped off earlier had two black bras, one pair of orange knickers, a bright pleated skirt and a sheer pastel flowery blouse."

"Don't blame me, they're your clothes."

The girls sent John away in search of magazines. Stella removed the clothes John had selected from the locker and replaced them with the ones she'd chosen and wondered how to raise the subject of Luigi. She sat on her friend's bed.

"Daffs, I'm so sorry."

"What for? This isn't your fault and I'll be OK."

"You came to make sure I was all right and I was. If I hadn't called you, that bloke would probably still have cleared off but without pushing you downstairs or whatever it was he did to put you in here."

"I don't remember what happened, just that you called me and I opened the street door under your flat. After that, it's all a blank."

"I know, but apparently that's quite common when people are knocked out."

"Stella, maybe I was given your blood? You've saved my life," Daphne said.

"The chances of you getting mine must be pretty small."

"Yes, but I needed five pints during my operation so it's possible. Anyway, if you'd fainted or something and hadn't got the ambulance so quickly I might have bled to death so you really did save my life."

"You're a great mate to see it that way. Maybe I should thank the gypsy for influencing you so you didn't realise it was me who put you at risk to start with."

"Not your fault. It was fate."

"Maybe. Like it was fate that one of us would end up with a tall, dark, handsome fella?"

"You've heard from Doug?"

"No. I'm talking about Luigi."

"Luigi?"

"Not me and Luigi, you and Luigi."

"Ah. But..."

"It's OK, mate."

"Nothing's happened."

"I know, but only because you were worried about what I'd think. Well, I think you're crazy about him and he's crazy about you. Or maybe you're both just crazy. Whatever."

"I thought you'd be upset."

"I would have been if I hadn't spoken to him today. Not because I went out with him; didn't we promise each other we'd never fall out over a man?"

"Yes, but..."

"No buts, Daphne. Getting a decent bloke is hard enough, don't go making it extra difficult for yourself."

"You're one to talk!" Daphne turned to face Stella and winced with pain.

"Take it easy, Daffs. OK, I'm not doing so well on the romance front right now, but we're not talking about me. We're talking about you... and Luigi. I'm fine about you seeing him now I've spoken to him."

"Really?"

"Yes. We were never meant to be. I know you thought we were because of the fortune telling, but it was never quite right. He's great fun and gorgeous looking, but I never really took it seriously. As I was telling John, Luigi didn't do anything wrong."

"You and my brother had a heart to heart?"

"Yes." Stella made sure that Daphne's jug of water was turned at an angle that would make it easy for her to grasp the handle and straightened the box of tissues. "He's nicer than I realised."

"Stella?"

"Yes, mate."

"It was true what the gypsy said, wasn't it? My job, you saving my life, our lives entwined."

"Could be."

"So the rest will be true. I knew it." Daphne seemed to be talking to herself and her eyes were closing.

"You get some rest. Would you like Luigi to come in later?'

"Please."

When John returned with magazines and chocolate, his sister was already asleep. "She's looking so frail, I'm worried about her."

"The doctors said she'll be fine," Stella said.

John put his purchases in Daphne's locker, kissed his sister's forehead and then he and Stella walked away.

"The break was nasty and her knee has been badly damaged, she'll need months of physiotherapy before she can walk properly," John said.

"She won't like that, you know the only time she sits still is when she's reading those flipping horoscopes," Stella said.

"Yeah. Mum wants Daphne to stay with her which I think is a good idea."

"I agree, your parents will spoil her rotten, but they'll make sure she does her physio and gets plenty of rest."

"Oh crikey; she's going to do those star charts she never had time for and she'll read every book she can on the subject. We'll just have to make that work in our favour. The gypsy who wrote that letter... the fortunes she gave you both were all good weren't they?"

"Yes, but you don't believe in all that, surely?" Stella asked.

"I don't have to; Daphne does. We can make her believe it's all coming true. If she believes in your tall, dark, handsome stranger, she'll also believe in the bit about walking down the aisle next to you; not being pushed in a wheelchair."

"That's brilliant, John. She was just telling me she does think it could all come true now, but I think she was just trying to convince herself. I'll remind her about getting the job and she seems to believe our being blood donors counts for the saving her life bit. I'll try and remember other stuff from the fortune... Oh hang on, you've got the letter, let's read that and see if it helps."

"It won't," John said, holding the ward door open for Stella.

"Oh?"

"You two are going to keep to your pact. Can you imagine how upset she'd be if she found out you hadn't."

"All right, but it doesn't say anything bad, does it?"

"Doesn't matter as you don't believe in any of it, do you? No, don't worry," John said and squeezed her hand.

Climbing down the concrete staircase, Stella realised she had been worrying.

"Maybe the gypsy cursed us because I laughed at her?

"Stella, you're getting yourself into a state. Come here." He pulled her against him and tilted her chin so she was looking at him. "There's no curse and the letter doesn't say anything bad, just nothing suitable for our purposes," John reassured her.

When he held her and looked into her eyes like that she could almost imagine what it would have been like if they'd never had that stupid row and he hadn't dumped her. Then she remembered how he'd spelled out his lack of interest in her when she'd dared to make a joke, outside her police taped flat, suggesting she thought he fancied her. She wasn't going to make that mistake again. She pulled herself away from his embrace.

"I hope you're right. Are you allowed to say how your investigation is going?"

"What investigation?"

"You're kidding me right? Your sister is badly injured and you've forgotten all about trying to catch the man who did it, surely you can see that catching him would make her feel safer? Me too, but I wouldn't expect you to care about that."

"I hadn't forgotten, no. It's just that there's not much evidence that anyone else was there."

"You aren't suggesting I pushed her?"

"Of course not. Don't be stupid, Stella. It's just that we have to consider that it may have been an accident. Daphne doesn't remember what happened and you told me you'd been dreaming about an intruder."

"So you think I made it all up?"

"No. Come on, please don't let us argue over this. I believe you are sure there was someone there and I promise I'll keep looking into it. Can we call a truce and trust each other to do whatever we can to help Daphne?"

He had a nerve, of course she'd help Daphne. Stella sighed; she knew John would help his sister too and he'd do the job properly. Why did she always over-react to anything he said or did?

"OK. We'll stay in touch then."

"Yes, you've got my number, haven't you?"

Stella felt her face flame as she remembered his name in her address book, garlanded with hearts. "Yes, you so thoughtfully wrote it in my book. I suppose you noticed that it's the same one I had as a kid?"

"Of course I did. I remember buying it for you."

"Oh. Yes. I'm going to speak to Luigi and see if we can work out a sort of rota so Daphne gets plenty of visitors, but not too many at a time. We don't want to be tripping over each other at her bedside, do we?"

"I..."

"Exactly and we don't want her to go too long without a visitor so I'll let you know when that might be a problem. I suppose it's going to be best for Luigi and others from the restaurant to go early in the day and for me and others with normal jobs to go in the evening and... "

"I can fit myself in if there are any breaks left in the busy schedule you've arranged for her, right," John said.

"I didn't mean it like that, it's just that you work unusual hours and..."

"Yes, I do. I'd better get back to work. See you."

He strode off towards the car park, leaving Stella to wait for the bus home. What was wrong with him? Maybe, despite what he'd said he blamed her for what had happened to Daphne.

It started raining. She pulled her collar up as high as she could and studied the timetable, trying to work out how long she'd have to wait. Unless the last one was running late, she'd be shivering on the street for nearly an hour.

A car pulled into the bus stop, splashing water over her feet.

"Get in," John said.

She did, but only because her catching pneumonia would just add to Daphne's problems.

Stella remembered the time she and Daphne, on a whim inspired by Daphne's interpretation of her horoscope, had got caught in the rain seven miles from home and had to walk until John had come to their rescue. She'd looked bedraggled and John had laughed at her, but that had been so much better than her looking tired with worry and him not speaking to her. Why did everything to do with him have to be so awkward?

John didn't say another word, even when she muttered her thanks and slammed the car door outside her flat.

Chapter Seventeen

Luigi came into Clover's and asked Stella to make a bouquet for Daphne. "She will go home tomorrow, I would like to take flowers there."

"Home? I thought she was going to stay with her parents." Now she was going to have to redo her carefully organised visiting rota.

"Yes, home with her parents."

"Right." Of course she was and of course Stella would misunderstand anything any man said to her.

"Do you know which she likes best?" he asked.

Which of her parents? No, flowers. She really should get a grip.

"Yes," she said, pointing out a variety of flowers she knew Daphne liked. It was easy, Daphne loved them all. Mr Clover allowed Stella to take home any blooms that had been in the shop for a few days as they wouldn't last long in customers' vases.

"A disappointed customer will rarely come back," he'd told her.

Stella had shared the flowers with Daphne who'd always been delighted and often made cakes or cookies for Stella in return. Stella would have given Daphne flowers anyway, but the cookies probably encouraged her to be slightly more generous.

Luigi plucked stems from each bucket of flowers that Stella indicated. "Will you make the bouquet yourself Stella, please?"

"Of course."

"Use these and as many others as you can get a ribbon around." He signed a cheque, leaving it blank for Stella to fill in the total once she'd worked out the cost. His faith that she wouldn't cheat him made her feel even worse about her own suspicions of him.

Stella arranged her next visit to Daphne brilliantly. Firstly she travelled by bus so she didn't have to inconvenience Daphne's irritable brother. Secondly, she timed her arrival so her conversation on the gypsy's prophecy came immediately after Luigi had visited and delivered the enormous bouquet.

"I hate to admit it, but that gypsy sure was right about a lot of things, too many to be coincidence. Trio is the number three that's been lucky for you after you got a job to do with food. I wonder what it says in that letter. Do you think it's Luigi's name and your wedding date?"

"Luigi's never mentioned marriage and that was before...." Daphne trailed off and pointed to her leg in its plaster cage.

"He's crazy about you and the odd small scar which is all you'll end up with won't put him off. It all fits, doesn't it? If you hadn't wanted to take care of me, you wouldn't have got injured by my burglar and if we weren't worried about health then we wouldn't be blood donors and I couldn't have saved your life."

"So it's all true? I'm going to get better and you'll find someone and we'll be each other's bridesmaids and friends forever?"

"Yes, I just need to find myself a new tall, dark, handsome man as you've snaffled the last one."

"Stella, I'm so sorry about that..."

"It's OK, really. I never believed in fate, but now I think there might be something in it. You two were obviously meant to be together. Your injuries have certainly brought out the best in Luigi; he's realised he doesn't want to risk losing you and sorted himself out. Look at the hours he's spent sat by your bed reading you the gossip columns and short stories from the magazines. Trust me, I did get to know him well enough to see he's now a changed man."

"He has been very kind."

"Yes."

That killed the conversation. Perhaps the kindness of Luigi towards Daphne was another thing the two of them might not choose to discuss in too much detail.

"My parents have been great too, but I'll be going home to my flat soon. I want to get back to normal and it'll help to be there. Not so far for you to travel to visit either."

"Great." Maybe Daphne wasn't as well as she thought if she'd prefer John scowling constantly to their mum serving cakes every twenty minutes. Or maybe there was less cake and scowling when Stella wasn't around.

"Stella, I'm starting to get my memory back, you know about my accident? That's if it was an accident."

"What do you mean?"

"I don't think I fell. It's difficult... the counsellor I've been speaking to thinks that I repressed the memory because of the shock. I'm sure your theory about a burglar is right and he pushed me down the stairs as he ran away. I'll tell John."

Stella rang John as soon as she left his parents' home. His investigation might not be going well, but at least she was keeping her part of the bargain.

"The plan went perfectly, she's convinced it's her fate to get better quickly. What's stage two?"

"You liked my mate Doug?"

"Yeah, nice bloke."

"And tall, dark, and handsome?"

"Ah, I'm with you. I pretend to go out with him."

"More than pretend. He's been pestering me about you since the party."

"Why would he do that? He's not made any attempt to contact me since except for a Christmas card at work."

"He's been very busy and he probably thought you'd call him."

"How could I? I don't have his number."

"Oh dear, did I forget to give it to you? Sorry about that."

What a rat, even over the phone she could tell he was lying. He didn't forget and he wasn't sorry.

"I thought you gave him my number?"

"Er, yes. Maybe I made a mistake with it, I'll check."

She had to disconnect the call to stop herself swearing at the man. What on earth was wrong with John? He'd made it perfectly clear he wasn't interested in her as a girlfriend but she had thought they'd finally made friends. Did he really think she was so horrible he'd needed to protect his friend from her?

Hopefully things would work out between her and Doug, and then John would be driven crazy by Doug constantly singing her praises.

John called and said he'd spoken to Doug and his friend was willing to go out with Stella. He phrased it as though Doug deserved a medal for this.

"OK, so where do I meet him?"

"Are you crazy? I know what you're like if anyone tries to arrange anything for you without asking first. There's no way I'd risk you throwing a tantrum."

Stella gritted her teeth. "I don't like people planning my life, it's true. Dating Doug was my idea though, remember? I didn't want you to set a date for the wedding, just arrange for us to have a drink together sometime."

"OK, I'll call you back."

He rang off before she could say it'd be easier to give her Doug's number and vice versa so they could make their own arrangements.

John called back half an hour later and said he'd arranged for Doug to meet her for a coffee on Saturday morning. Maybe John had forgotten she worked Saturdays, but she wasn't sure about that. Arguing with him over the arrangements would just be petty though. She'd show him she wasn't going to be dragged down to his level.

"Fine, I'll ask Mr Clover if I can take my lunch break early. It shouldn't be a problem to go at about eleven."

"Right. I'll tell Doug to meet you in the coffee shop then, shall I?" He disconnected the call before she could agree or otherwise.

Although she got up half an hour early, Stella had to run to work. It had taken her far longer than she'd anticipated to get dressed in a way that wouldn't shock Mr Clover and the ladies buying flowers for the church, but which would still make an impression on Doug. She settled for black trousers and a skimpy, slinky top that she could cover with a nice sensible cardigan.

The walk between the florist's and the coffee shop wasn't far, but it was cold. Deciding goose bumps weren't a sexy look, she went straight in even though there was no sign of Doug. The warm air that enveloped her was scented with the most delicious coffee aroma. Stella ordered a cappuccino; Doug was sure to be there by the time her drink was ready.

He hadn't arrived by the time she'd finished it. She had to eat or she'd be chewing the roses in the shop by five o'clock. If this was some scheme of John's to annoy her she wasn't going to let it get to her. Thanks to a small pay rise from Mr Clover she could afford to treat herself to a duck and hoisin wrap, a white chocolate and macadamia nut cookie and another cappuccino.

Looking at the empty place opposite her she decided the tables were too bare and would benefit from a small vase of flowers. Perhaps just three white carnations to tone in with a more elaborate arrangement on the sleek dark counter. She'd come back in the week with a brochure, order book; and a more appropriate top.

She'd been in there recently with John; why hadn't she noticed then that the place was another potential customer for Clover's? It certainly wasn't because his stunning looks had captured her attention, but at least he'd arrived on time.

A cold draft made her shiver as the door opened. Doug rushed in and the sight of his big brown eyes and tight, but not too tight, brown trousers warmed her up again.

"Wow, you look fantastic! Until a few moments ago, I'd been thinking what a dull grey day it was," he said.

He was forgiven.

"Hi, Doug. Glad you could make it."

"Sorry, Stella, have you been waiting long?" he asked as he looked at the empty coffee mug and plate in front of her. "John said you'd be meeting me in your lunch break."

"I just bet he did."

"Is something wrong?"

"Not at all, I think there's been a mix up though as I thought we were meeting earlier and I have to be back at work in about fifteen minutes." Moaning about her date's best mate before he'd even sat down probably wouldn't be the best way to impress him.

"Oh, that's a shame. I'll order us both a coffee and we'll talk fast, how's that?"

"Great." She'd never actually heard of anyone dying from cappuccino overdose.

"Nice top," he said as he returned with the drinks. "Where did you get it? Monsoon?"

"Phase 8 actually."

"Nice."

A man who understood clothes? She glanced down at his feet; clearly he understood shoes too. Doug was so much nicer and better looking than John. Probably as good looking and charming as Luigi, except that she wasn't at all interested in either him or John and absolutely refused to make comparisons. Maybe this time she'd end up with a decent boyfriend? She was getting ahead of herself though. She wasn't at all sure if he'd been persuaded by John to come because of the gypsy's prophecy or because he really was interested in her.

"I know I've only just got here, but can I see you again?" Doug asked.

"Er, yes, I suppose."

"Sorry, to spring that on you, but as we're so short of time I pretty much have to work fast."

"Of course. Well, I'm not working tomorrow, so you can take me out for lunch if you like." Two could play at working fast and it would save her having to play happy families with Luigi and John at Trio.

"I'd love to," Doug said. "Unfortunately I do have to work. How do you feel about pub quizzes?"

"I'm not sure I have an opinion."

"Come with me to The Frog and Bucket on Wednesday night then? My team I and know nothing about flowers."

At least he hadn't forgotten everything about her.

"Sure, love to."

"Could I check I have your right number, Stella?" he asked after they'd agreed a time. "I tried ringing the one John gave me, but just got a bloke called Big Steve who was convinced I wanted to buy a motorbike."

Stella gave him her number.

"Ah, I had double two three, not two double three. I can't trust John."

"I know what you mean."

Chapter Eighteen

When Stella arrived at The Frog and Bucket, wearing the even skimpier cousin of the top she'd worn the last time she'd seen him, Doug was waiting outside for her. He bent and kissed her cheek.

"Great to see you. And I have to say you're looking great."

"Thanks. I didn't know if this top was a bit much?" What she really meant was she didn't know if there should be a bit more of it.

"Not at all. Looks great with those jeans too. Diesel aren't they, like mine?" He turned so she could see the label.

"Yes. I got them from TK Maxx, absolute bargain."

"Me too!" He reached for her hand. "Come on and I'll introduce you to the guys you don't already know."

"That'll be all of them, I expect." She never drank in The Frog and Bucket.

"Except for John, of course."

"Of course." Why hadn't it occurred to her that John would be one of his team mates?

"That's not a problem is it?" he asked as he led the way through the busy pub.

"No." She knew how she'd feel if Doug told her he didn't like Daphne.

"Stella, meet Luke and Simon. Guys, this is Stella, she's our expert on flowers and chocolate."

"Bit sexist, that mate, isn't it? Assuming that a girl only knows about stuff like that," Luke said as he shuffled down the bench to make room for her.

"Not sexist, Stella-ist," John said. "Trust us, if the question is about either of those subjects, Stella's our man."

"My round. What'll you have, Stella?" Simon asked.

There was an awkward pause in the conversation when he left for the bar. Stella picked up the glass dish of flowers from the table.

"Nice gerberas. Don't you think they go well with the asparagus fern, variegated euonymus and star chrysanthemums?" She'd known that wasn't likely to be a quiz question, but she was still glad she'd paid attention to the names when she'd calculated the bill for the pub. "I work in Clover's florist's," she told Luke in case the poor guy thought she sat at home doing flower arrangements instead of going to work.

"She handles all the marketing as well as designing arrangements. Almost any flowers you see looking good in town will be there because of Stella," John said.

What he said was basically true, but it sounded much more dynamic than trudging round businesses with a brochure and then sticking cut stems into dishes of Oasis. If he was trying to make friends he was doing a great job.

The first question was about football and the second on cars, so Stella didn't have to even pretend she was thinking of an answer. Luke insisted on analysing each question even though it was clear the other three all agreed on the answer. The third was, "milk chocolate contains 20 per cent of what toxic substance?"

Stella started to speak, but was interrupted by Luke.

"That has to be a trick question, chocolate isn't toxic."

"It is if you have too much," John said.

"So is anything," Simon pointed out.

"Then the answer must be milk. Stands to reason, the clue is in the question."

"It's cocoa," Stella eventually managed to say.

John wrote her answer on the score card.

"I don't think that can be right. Doesn't chocolate have to contain much more than that? I was reading an article about EU law in The Independent..."

Fortunately they were saved from hearing about it by a question on Star Wars. Simon knew that one. The next one was, 'Which sign of the zodiac would you fall under if your birthday was during the first week of January.'

"Stella, do you know that one?" Luke asked.

Stella looked up and saw John grinning at her.

"Can I phone a friend?" she asked and both she and John began to laugh.

"Capricorn," she said at last. She should know as Daphne's birthday was in January and Stella had therefore been forced to read out the horoscope for that sign every day since Daphne's accident two weeks ago. Reading one version to Daphne wasn't so bad, but searching through every paper and magazine in the newsagents to find one that was suitable to read was driving her crazy.

By the time the quiz master collected the sheets, they had an answer in every space and agreed on the team name Stellar Cops. Stella also knew where Doug had bought his shoes and shirt and who'd designed them.

The boys had been right about the football and car questions and congratulated each other.

"Oh well done, Stella," Luke said as the answer to the chocolate question was read out.

They cheered or groaned until all the answers had been confirmed. There was a lot more cheering than groaning. Their team came second, winning a free round of drinks and Stella promised she'd join them again the following Saturday. Doug walked her home, which would probably have been a whole lot better if it hadn't been for John remembering something he had to discuss with Doug and coming with them.

Doug rang her the following day to try to arrange to take her to dinner, but they couldn't find a date they were both free. Stella was very busy visiting Daphne, planning displays for Clover's or watching a really interesting series on TV.

Doug didn't seem particularly disappointed. "How about the next quiz night? Can you make that?"

"Yes, I think so. I'll see you there."

When the Valentine's display went up in Clover's window at the end of January, it was Stella who chose the backdrop, flowers and accessories and decided where they'd go. Mr Clover acted as her assistant, lugging buckets of long stemmed red roses and a gilded harp.

"That looks wonderful, Stella," he said as soon as he'd got his breath back.

"It does, doesn't it?" Stella opened the door to the shop for Mr Clover. "Although I probably shouldn't say so myself."

"It's good that you recognise your achievements and you have achieved a lot since you've been working for me. Here, take this and go and buy us a cream cake each. I think we deserve a treat after all our hard work." He gave her five pounds from the till.

When Stella returned, Mr Clover was still resting in the chair he'd sat in when they'd come back into the shop. He started to stand. "Sorry, I should have put the kettle on."

"That's OK, I'll do it."

She made their drinks and carried them in to the shop.

"Stella, I've been thinking... I'm really getting too old for shifting buckets, doing the deliveries and working six days a week."

"But you can't close the shop! Look how well we're doing and we've got advance bookings for weddings this summer. We can't let people down. I can do more..."

He held up a hand. "Stella, Stella, it's all right, I'm not thinking of closing. Quite the opposite. I thought maybe we could recruit someone to help us. They could do the deliveries and all the fetching and carrying and once we'd trained them up they could help out when you took your holidays or I felt like a day off."

"Oh, I see." Mr Clover hadn't ever taken a holiday or more than an hour off for medical or dental appointments in the whole time she'd worked for him. Why had she never noticed that before?

"We'll have to be very careful it's someone we both think is suitable. Since you've been here, it's been a very pleasant place to work. I wouldn't want that to change."

"Hmm, unless we already know them, I'm not sure how we'd tell what they were like."

"It's difficult."

"What about if we took someone on temporarily and then if we liked them, offer them a permanent position?"

"Good idea, perhaps you could start advertising? Assistance during the next few weeks would be most useful."

Stella was elated to have taken part in her first management decision; maybe she was turning into a grown-up at last?

John hardly spoke to Stella as he drove them to visit Daphne at his parents' home.

"Did you tell Daphne about me going to the quiz with Doug?" she asked.

"No."

"Oh. I thought you would."

"I didn't. Is there much to tell?"

There wasn't as she was sure he knew. "But that was the idea, so she'd think the fortune thing was coming true. I'm sure she'll be pleased."

"Probably."

"I'll tell her then, shall I?"

"Right."

Stella reported to her friend how much she'd enjoyed her date with Doug and that they'd arranged to go out again. She didn't mention that both dates were to the quiz evenings, partly because she didn't trust herself to mention John without revealing her irritation.

"Brilliant, so what do your stars say?" Daphne asked.

"Mine?" Help, she hadn't vetted hers. Still, it was unlikely they'd say anything specific enough that Stella couldn't convince Daphne that it didn't apply to her.

"*You've been worried lately, but for no reason.* Oooh, that must be about you. I was worried, but you're doing so well, I don't need to. *Turn your attentions to something positive.* I wonder what they mean by that?"

"Work? Is that going well?" Daphne asked.

"It is. Really well actually. We're going to employ someone else to help. Hopefully they'll do most of the deliveries to customers and the heavy stuff in the shop and serving when I have a day off or am out trying to get more business."

"Sounds good."

"I'm really hoping he or she can start straight away and do the Valentine's deliveries. We've got loads of orders for businesses as well as the bouquets and red roses and stuff that you'd expect and it'll be really busy in the shop. I'm making sure we have cheaper posies as well as the pricey stuff so the blokes who usually only splash out once a year will see that flowers don't have to cost an arm and a leg and some of them might come back more often."

"Stella, that's great."

"Well, you'd expect a florist to be busy at the start of February."

"I didn't really mean that. It's your enthusiasm. You didn't ever talk about work except to moan about working Saturdays; now you sound like I do when we're considering adding a new dish to the menu."

"Yes, I suppose you're right."

"And Doug, you really like him?"

"Yes, I do." She made sure she sounded as enthusiastic as she had when discussing work. The last thing she wanted was for Daphne to be worried about her and if she were to admit that, although Doug was good looking and very charming, she just didn't fancy him now she'd started to get to know him then Daphne might well be concerned.

The Stellar Cops team again came second at the quiz. Doug again discussed nothing other than the quiz questions and their clothes. That wasn't fair; they didn't really have the opportunity to have a proper conversation and he did manage to tell her what make of car he owned. It didn't mean anything to her, but she gathered it would be appropriate to look impressed.

She sighed. He was a nice enough bloke, but she really couldn't persuade herself she was interested in him at all. He looked good and thought she did too, but there didn't seem to be much below the surface. She'd have to let him down gently, then face John and explain she couldn't go through with their plan.

Doug again walked her home, this time John didn't come with them. Instead, just as Stella and Doug reached her front door and Doug had bent his head as though to kiss her, John phoned him.

"Hi John... Really?... You're sure?... What, right now?...OK," Doug said at intervals.

"I'm really sorry, Stella, but there's been a development in the case, I have to go."

"Case?"

"Your prowler or whatever he was. Seems he's struck again."

"And, even though you're both off-duty, John has discovered this in the five minutes since we left the pub?" Stella was furious. If John was now actively investigating the case, why on earth hadn't he told her?

"Apparently. I really have to go, but can I buy you lunch tomorrow?"

He already knew she could take an hour's break from work so she had no reason to refuse. Besides, it was nice to have admiring male company. "Er, OK."

Doug gave her a quick kiss and was gone.

"What are you grinning at?" she demanded of Thirteen when she got in. Obviously, as a male, he just sat there looking good and was of no help whatsoever.

The following day, Stella took care not to dress at all provocatively and spent the morning trying to think of tactful ways to tell Doug that she didn't want to see him again.

"Hi Stella, are you cold?" Doug asked as soon as she walked into the coffee shop.

Perhaps she'd overdone covering up her assets?

"What's wrong? You don't look happy. Do you have a cold or something?"

For a moment it crossed her mind to say she wasn't well and so couldn't go out with him, but that would only be a temporary solution. In any case, he deserved the truth.

The waitress arrived to take their order. The extra thinking time didn't help.

"Doug, I er, this is a bit awkward," Stella said as soon as the girl had left to fetch their sandwiches.

"Don't worry, John has already explained."

"He has?"

"Yes. He said you're not looking to get too serious right now, concentrating on your career at the florist's is your priority for the moment. "

That was partly true and she rather wished she'd thought of it, but why on earth did John say it? He knew how she felt about having her life organised and surely had no idea how she felt about Doug.

"You just want us to be friends, is that right, Stella?"

She nodded. Annoyingly, John's explanation was a lot better than anything she'd thought of.

"Promise you'll stay on our quiz team though? Me and the guys don't have a clue about the celebrity and horoscope questions or anything to do with plants or chocolate."

"Of course." Attending the quizzes would allow her to keep up the pretence of the tall, dark boyfriend.

She couldn't think of anything else to say until the waitress returned with their order.

"Friends?" he said, holding his drink as though giving a toast.

"Yes, friends," Stella said and bumped her coffee cup against his.

"Thank goodness for that!"

Her surprise must have shown because he immediately apologised.

"I didn't mean it like that. You're lovely, Stella. I like you a lot but I'm busy with my career too and likely to move soon. A serious relationship isn't what I want just now."

"I understand." She did; he wasn't any more interested in her than she was in him.

"I really would like us to be friends though. Would it work, do you think?"

"We could try. Actually, it would be great if we can. You see..." How could she explain she'd only gone out with him to make a horoscope come true?

"Sounds like you have a confession to make. To make it easier for you, I'll go first. When I agreed to be your blind date at that party, I did it to annoy John. Of course once I'd checked you out in the flower shop I was glad I'd said yes..."

"I thought John was your friend?"

"He is, but he isn't half annoying. He's got a real thing about you and reckons he knows what's best for everyone so the minute he suggested I might not want to go along with his sister's plan, I decided I would."

Stella grinned at him. If Doug found John irritating and wanted to get back at him for that, they had a lot more in common than she realised. She explained the reason for John finally allowing Doug and Stella to date.

"I like Daphne and I'll be glad to help. But, maybe John doesn't need to know that?"

"We pretend we're, well, more than friends?"

They giggled together as they ate and imagined how annoyed John would be to hear Doug telling him what a wonderful girl Stella was and how happy they were together.

Obviously Stella couldn't tell Daphne about her pact with Doug. She didn't mention the investigation either. She was sure John would keep his sister informed and he'd do it more tactfully than she could. She also failed to mention that John turned up on half her dates with Doug and when he wasn't actually with them he'd just happen to be passing when Doug took her home and invite himself to share the coffee she'd offered Doug, or would call Doug just as he was about to kiss her goodnight to say there were developments on a case and Doug was needed urgently at the station.

She certainly didn't mention that she was really pleased about this as it showed just how much her 'relationship' with Doug was irritating John.

Chapter Nineteen

Every couple of days, John rang to ask if Stella would like a lift to his flat to see Daphne.

"The doctors are really pleased with Daphne's progress," John told her during one journey. "They think she'll eventually walk without a limp at all, although once the cast comes off she'll need lots of physio."

"And how is she, you know, other than her leg?"

"Fine. She's not getting tired like she was the first few days after she left hospital. Best of all, Luigi is keeping her occupied so she doesn't get bored and start fretting." John laughed. "Don't look like that. I meant when he wasn't with her. He leaves recipes for her to look at, things to taste and paperwork for her to do, so she's still able to do some work. He's promised she can come in and supervise the cooking as soon as she's ready. It's been a real job to convince her to wait a bit longer."

"And our plan about Rosie-Lee's mumbo jumbo, it that doing any good?"

"It's working, Stella," John said. "After she's finished raving about how lovely Luigi is to her, she tells me how happy she is for you. I'm just glad that gypsy didn't mention me in that fortune of yours."

"Watch your step, or I might suddenly remember she said you'd start ballet lessons and learn to speak Russian."

"You wouldn't?"

"OK, maybe not. It's bad enough for me."

"What do you mean; isn't it working out with Doug? He seems quite keen."

Ooops, she'd nearly blurted out the truth. "Huh! Like I'd get a chance to find out with you as chaperone or constantly phoning to drag him away." And telling Doug she wasn't interested. What had that all been about?

"Ah. Yes, he did say I usually call at precisely the right moment. Er, wrong moment, I mean."

"Yes."

"Stella, about Doug... You might have noticed that he's not exactly the deep and sensitive type."

"Not with you, perhaps," she said. Luckily they'd reached his place by then and she was able to flounce off to see Daphne and leave him to wonder what that meant.

She wished she could share the truth with Daphne. She wanted to talk through John's weird behaviour with someone. He was behaving just like a jealous ex-boyfriend. She caught herself wondering what might have happened between them if he'd never walked in to hear her and Daphne talking that time. They'd been discussing what they'd wear at the imagined wedding between Stella and John which would transform the two girls into the sisters Daphne so much wanted them to be. Silly to think of that now and pointless too, Daphne was already her sister in spirit if not in law.

Somewhere there must be a kind, decent man who shared the same interests and outlook as Stella. Surely that wasn't just a romantic dream?

Stella put a sign advertising the job vacancy in the window at Clover's and printed out a handful of application forms.

These were soon requested by girls; one was chewing gum, one sported nose and other face piercings and another was accompanied by a screaming baby.

"Can you drive?" Stella asked each in turn and was relieved when the first eventually removed the headphones from her ears, asked Stella to repeat the question and then said she was too young. The one with the baby couldn't afford lessons, but Stella had to wait until she'd finished answering her mobile to learn that. The one with the potentially customer scaring piercings had a medical condition which meant she couldn't drive.

"I'm sorry, but you're not quite what we're looking for. We really do need someone with a full, clean driving licence," she told them each in turn.

Stella intended to take her test soon, so might cope with the deliveries herself. What she couldn't cope with was trying to train a girl who ignored the block capitals stating 'full clean driving licence essential' that she'd printed on the advert and who couldn't even manage to seem interested in the job during the short time it took to ask for the application form.

Mr Clover and Stella made a few enquiries amongst their customers about the possibility of employing someone local.

One lady said, "My neighbour has recently taken early retirement and he told me the other day that he's regretting it a bit as he's bored being at home all the time and thinks he's getting under his wife's feet. I'll mention it to him."

Less than an hour later, the man himself arrived and requested an application form.

"To be honest, my old job was stressful. I like the idea of getting about doing deliveries with nothing more to worry about than getting the right bouquet to the right person on time."

Mr Clover booked him in for an interview on the twelfth of February. Pete started working the same day. Mr Clover took him around the premises, showed him the van and explained his duties. On his second day, they did the deliveries together. The next morning, the men loaded the van. Pete was given a list of addresses and he set off to do the Valentine's deliveries, leaving Stella and Mr Clover to deal with those customers who'd left it to the last minute to buy flowers.

The postman brought in a gift wrapped box. "You've got an admirer, Stella," he said as he handed it over.

She ripped off the paper to reveal a box of classy chocolates. Stuck to the top was a square of paper bearing printed words. 'Something nearly as sweet as you from your boy in blue,' she read to the interested looking postman. How kind of Doug. She'd have to find a way to make sure John saw it.

At eleven o'clock, Pete walked back into the shop carrying a huge bouquet of gorgeous roses. Stella remembered assembling it. She'd made just two of the most extravagant bouquets she'd listed in Clover's new brochure. One had been ordered by Luigi for Daphne. As Stella had snipped and tweaked the stems, she'd fantasised that she'd one day impress a man enough that he'd want to send her an armful of roses and exotic foliage. It seemed her life was like her job as far as romance was concerned. She worked to prepare the flowers, but was left with a pile of thorns and scruffy leaves whilst someone else got nice clean stems and beautiful blooms.

"Pete, you really shouldn't take them out of the boxes until you actually deliver them, in case they get damaged."

"No, of course not, but..."

"What's wrong, can't you find the address?"

"There isn't one."

"There must be." As she said it she recalled the list Mr Clover had written out and the flowers she'd put ready for deliveries. There had been a lot, so it wasn't so hard to believe one of them might have made a mistake.

"There's a card, does it have a name?" she asked. With luck that would give them a clue.

Pete already had his hands full, so Stella picked up the tiny envelope and saw her own name neatly printed on the outside.

"Someone has great taste," Pete said and winked at her before handing over the flowers and going out to continue the deliveries.

Inside the card was written, 'Roses are red, violets are blue. You're loved but you don't know by who'.

The writer was correct, she didn't know. The flowers couldn't possibly be from Doug. If he'd felt strongly enough to send them he'd have tried harder to continue their relationship. Luke or Simon from the quiz team? Unlikely. They were both friendly, and complimented her in a jokey way but neither had ever asked her out or given any hint that they were romantically interested in her.

She picked up the card from the chocolates and read it again. Did it say boy in blue, or boys? Yes, boys. The whole team must have sent it as a joke; very appropriate as chocolate was her specialist subject. Poor John, bet his pint tasted bitter when they suggested the idea.

That still didn't explain the flowers. Though both messages were hand printed, the letters were formed differently and whilst one made it reasonably clear who the sender was, the other didn't give a clue at all. Which other men did she know? Luigi? No way, he was crazy about Daphne and even if he did want to be nice to Stella, he wouldn't risk doing so in a way that she could interpret as being disloyal to Daphne. Pete was happily married and hardly knew her. An ex-boyfriend who'd seen the error of his ways? Her landlord, dentist, the man who cleaned the shop windows? Perhaps it was a secret admirer she was completely unaware of. That idea was the least appealing. Stella shivered at the idea someone could be watching her.

She studied the card again, maybe she'd misread that one too. She hadn't.

She wouldn't have to wonder for long though; as she hadn't taken the order, that only left Mr Clover. Not as the sender, even she wasn't daft enough to guess he fancied her. He did like her though and would have been pleased to know she had an admirer.

"You didn't tell me when I was making these up that they were for me."

"No. That would have spoiled the surprise, wouldn't it?" Mr Clover said.

"I suppose. So, who are they from?"

"I can't tell you."

"You don't know?" That didn't seem possible. Even if the order was placed by phone, the customer would have had to give his name when he made the credit card payment.

"I do know, but as you've read the card and found it unsigned, I imagine he wishes to remain anonymous."

"Doug sent me these chocolates." She was nearly sure that was partly true.

"How kind of him."

"Yes. Even kinder if he sent the flowers too."

"Yes, if it were he."

"And was it?"

"Come now, Stella, I can't tell you that. If I were to say yes, that would deprive him of his anonymity and if I were to say it wasn't, I think that would also give the game away."

Actually it wouldn't help much, but any information would be better than none. "Did he arrive by police car?"

"I shan't tell you, Stella."

"Then I'll assume they were from you," she teased, hoping that would get a response.

"If they were, I'd have made up the bouquet myself."

That was true.

Later, when he saw her studying the cheques that were due to be banked, he admitted the sender of the roses paid in cash, but that was the nearest he came to giving her a clue.

Exactly six weeks after being rushed into hospital, Daphne had the cast removed from her leg. She did have a scar, but it was small and would fade in time. Daphne seemed more concerned that Luigi who'd taken her to the hospital, had seen her leg unshaven and as pale and spindly as an oven ready chicken.

"Oh that explains it!" John said after hearing Daphne moan to Stella about the humiliation.

"Explains what?" she demanded.

"Why I spotted Luigi running up and down the High Street screaming, 'save me from Daphne Drumstick.'"

Stella had to pretend to cough to hide her laughter.

"You think I'm over-reacting?" Daphne asked.

"Not at all. He'll probably make a Daphne Drumstick cocktail and serve it with scrawny white straws dangling over the side of the glass."

This time Stella couldn't disguise her amusement. "I'm afraid John's right. Seeing your left leg not looking quite as perfect as the right one isn't going to scare Luigi off. It's not important and anyway, it's only temporary. A bit of exercise and some fake tan and it'll be as good as new."

Much more important was that the break had healed and Daphne could walk. Her first physiotherapy appointment was scheduled for the following day. Daphne would be returning to work in Trio's kitchens just as soon as Luigi was assured it was safe for her to do so.

Chapter Twenty

Work was busy for Stella. Pete took care of all the deliveries, both from suppliers and to customers. That meant Mr Clover could cope with manning the counter and chatting to regulars and Stella was able to concentrate on advertising leaflets and speaking to prospective customers about flowers for businesses, parties and weddings.

Most of Stella's free time was taken up by travelling to Daphne and John's flat, encouraging Daphne with her physiotherapy, vetting horoscopes with John so Daphne saw only positive ones, planning with John to make the horoscopes come true and listening to Daphne tell her how wonderful Luigi was. Other than that, she attended the quizzes, watched quizzes on the television and read encyclopaedias she borrowed from the library. Maybe that's why she never bumped into her mystery admirer.

Luigi brought Daphne to Stella's flat. Once he was sure she was comfortably settled on Stella's sofa, he left them to talk.

"Notice anything different?" Daphne asked.

"You've come out without your stick."

"Yes, but I told you yesterday that I can walk without it now."

"You did, you've done really well. I'm proud of you."

"So is Luigi. When we were walking yesterday, he asked if I still needed to hold on to him and I said I didn't."

"Yeah, but I can't imagine either of you really wanted him to let go... Oh, Daphne has something happened?"

"It sure has. He let go of my arm, dropped to one knee and proposed!"

It was then that Stella noticed the glittering ring on Daphne's finger. She leapt up, grabbed Daphne and hugged her. "Congratulations, that's wonderful!"

"We haven't set a date or anything yet. He wants me to go with him to Italy and meet his family. Oh..."

"It's fine, Daffers, really. I'm very happy for you. I told you my relationship with Luigi never felt right, but with you it seems perfect."

"And you'll be my bridesmaid?"

"I will, of course I will."

The girls hugged again. Then Stella took a proper look at Daphne's ring. It was a delicate creation of white gold set with three square cut stones in the same vivid green as the four leafed clover earrings Luigi had given Stella for Christmas. Between each were tiny diamonds. The only thing brighter in Stella's flat was the sparkle in her friend's eyes.

"We should drink a toast to celebrate," Stella said.

"I like your thinking, but I'm not sure you've got a bottle of champagne in the fridge."

"I haven't, but I've still got some of that green stuff."

"Oh dear, do I have to?"

"Yes, Daphne my dear, you do; it's lucky."

Stella was happy for Daphne, but a little jealous too. Not because she was marrying Luigi, but because her best friend didn't seem to need her anymore. When Daphne announced in a phone call that she'd lost interest in horoscopes it felt as though the old Daphne had gone from her life forever.

"I don't need them. You were right Stella, they're just rubbish. The gypsy at the fairground told me all I need to know. It's all coming true for me and I know it will for you too."

"Yeah, course it will, mate. Talking of which, it's the quiz tonight and I'll have to leave in an hour. I'd better go and make myself look beautiful."

"What are you going to do for the other fifty-nine minutes?"

Stella laughed, "Put on a baggy top to hide my assets so I don't have the boys fighting over me?"

"How's it going with Doug, really?"

"Fine."

"As bad as that?"

"There's no fooling you, is there? We haven't fallen out or anything, it's just that we haven't fallen in love either."

"That's a shame. I want you to be as happy as I am."

"I'm fine, really, and I'm busy at work, so don't worry about me. Maybe it'll work out with the guy who sent me roses?"

"You still don't know who it was?"

"Nope."

"Maybe someone from your quiz team?"

"OK, what have you done with Daphne? My friend wouldn't torture me like this. I know I told you what those blokes are like, and you needn't think I was fooled by all that stuff about giving up the horoscopes."

"OK, I still read them, but honestly I don't need them now. I'm already living happily ever after."

Yes she was, unlike Stella who was just pretending.

After disconnecting, Stella spent fifty minutes trying on outfits and applying make-up before deciding she was trying way too hard for an evening with a bloke she didn't fancy, her mate's brother and a couple of social misfits who made up her quiz team.

She was glad she'd not gone to any trouble when she discovered both Doug and John had been called into work. The quiz was no fun without them and even her research was a waste of effort as it seemed that half the questions were on football and the rest about action movies. She got home safely, not that anyone cared.

The next day, John visited the florist's to ask her advice on the best choice of flowers to give a girl, "I really like, but don't want to scare off with loads of red roses or anything OTT."

Great, now he was laughing about her mystery admirer and couldn't even be bothered to get his facts right. The bloke, whoever he was, seemed to have scared himself off. Hilarious though, wasn't it, that Daphne was engaged, John had a girlfriend and poor old Stella had nobody.

"So, what shall I give her?" John prompted.

Stella bit her lip before she could suggest hemlock and poison ivy. Her job seemed to be all she had going for her; she couldn't risk it.

"How about freesias?" She tried not to think of a girl simpering at him as she accepted the pretty posy and how she'd think of his sweet gesture each time she smelt the lovely perfume.

"Perfect. Which colour would be best?"

"They're all nice. Get the colour you think she'd prefer."

"You know I'm rubbish at that sort of thing. Remember the clothes I took to Daphne in hospital?"

He really was hopeless. How was he ever going to pluck up the courage to hand them over to the poor girl? She wasn't being fair again. Doug could have picked some to co-ordinate with a girl's outfit but he'd have been more likely to make sure they complemented whatever he was wearing. With John, it would be the meaning rather than the actual gift that was important.

"The mauve and purple ones are very pretty."

"I'll take both, can you do them up with ribbon and stuff?"

John paid, picked out a gift card and began writing.

"I've got good news: we've arrested the bloke who we think broke into your flat and injured Daphne. We caught him on another job, but we're sure it's the same bloke," he said.

"Brilliant! Well done."

"I wondered if you could come and look at some mug-shots, just in case you've seen him hanging around?"

"Of course. I could come to the station in my lunch break. I doubt I'll be any help though."

"Maybe not, but it's worth a try."

John's radio demanded his attention and he left abruptly. Stella was about to pick up his flowers and go after him when she saw her name on the card. Inside it read, 'Sorry to stand you up yesterday, but we were catching the burglar. Will you come out to help me celebrate the arrest?'

Aaaaw sweet. Why was he asking by letter though; was she really so scary?

At the police station, John took her into an interview room and said, "I'm going to show you a selection of photographs of different men. One of them is of the man we believe pushed Daphne down your stairs."

She felt nervous which was completely ridiculous.

"All you've got to do is tell me if any of them look familiar."

"I can do that."

He turned over the pages in a flip file. In each plastic wallet were four different photographs. They all looked as though they were guilty of something, or did she just think that because of the circumstances?

"Oh!"

"Which one?"

"There, him. But John, I don't mean that he's the burglar."

"You've seen him before, though?"

"Yes." She fidgeted in her seat. She didn't like the man, but that was no reason to suggest he could be Daphne's attacker. Still, she needn't worry, if the creepy donkey jacket man were innocent then the police wouldn't be interested in him, especially as they already had a suspect.

"I've seen him hanging around outside my flat a few times. I thought he might be going to move in underneath me, but fortunately that never happened."

"You don't like him. Why?"

"I don't know really, he was just creepy."

"He didn't give you any trouble?"

"No. Anyway it doesn't matter, I haven't seen him lately."

"Would you like a cup of tea or anything?"

"No, it's OK. I'd better look at the rest of the photos and then get back to work."

John had closed the file.

"John, was that him? The man you arrested?"

"Yes. He hasn't been found guilty of anything yet, but yes, he's our suspect."

"How did you catch him?"

"He climbed into a woman's bedroom window and took her photograph while she slept. Luckily, a relation was staying with her that night and saw the flash. He tackled the bloke and held him down while he called us."

"Crikey."

"Luckily our suspect is a weedy asthmatic and the victim's relation is a semi-professional rugby player."

"So, what happens now?"

"I'll take another statement from you, if that's OK. Some of my colleagues are searching his house. We're guessing he takes photographs each time. If that's the case, we'll have evidence about the other places he broke into."

"In my dream, I thought I'd had my picture taken..."

"Yes."

"He really photographed me, didn't he?"

Stella shuddered and John put an arm around her shoulders.

"He might have done, yes."

"And then I woke up and called Daphne. He hid and then pushed her down the stairs so he could get away."

"Possibly." He gave her a brief hug before saying, "I'll be right back."

He opened the door, looked out and returned almost immediately. "Stella, this is Lucy, she's a victim support counsellor. I'll get you that tea now, shall I?"

Stella nodded and John left. Lucy sat down in the seat he'd vacated.

"Would you like to talk?" she asked.

Stella looked at Lucy's sensible grey bob, kindly blue eyes and sympathetic expression. If she wanted to talk, she was sure Lucy would listen. John must have arranged for her to be standing by, just in case she was needed.

By the time he returned, Stella felt calmer and had told the counsellor she was fine really.

"It was a shock and it's a horrible thought, but as John says, they've got him now. He won't be coming back to my flat."

Lucy had assured Stella she could ring anytime for a chat. "Take my card. If you want to talk about anything, please do call. It doesn't matter what it is, if it bothers you then it's worth calling me."

Stella doubted she'd want to call, but it was reassuring to know she could if she wanted. After Lucy had gone, Stella looked at the small card in her hand. It reminded her of the card John had once written out and attached to a bunch of flowers he'd bought from her. The tiny white envelope had born the name Lucy. Perhaps he'd purchased them for a colleague's birthday rather than as a gift for a girlfriend.

The afternoon at Clover's was busy, which suited her just fine. She didn't want time to think about that horrible man and his camera. She wasn't too keen on going back to her flat for a quiet evening either, so stayed late in the shop, working on another advertising leaflet. It was seven by the time she printed out a sample and left it on Mr Clover's desk.

John was standing outside when she finally closed the front door of the shop. It was only then she realised she hadn't said anything to him about his offer of a celebratory meal. She should have said something when she was in the police station, but she hadn't really had the chance. It didn't seem that this was the right time either. John didn't look as though he had good news.

Chapter Twenty-One

"What is it? Is Daphne OK?" Stella asked as she locked the door to Clover's.

"She's fine, don't worry. I thought you might offer me a cup of coffee." It was clear John wanted to talk, but wasn't going to do so on the street.

"OK."

He walked next to her, but didn't say a word. Even inside her flat, he waited to speak until she'd put the freesias he'd given her into water and filled the kettle.

"You're right, they do smell nice."

"They didn't scare me off, either," Stella said. She gave him a slight smile, but could see the time still wasn't right to arrange a dinner date.

John didn't speak again until they were both siting on her sofa with a hot drink. They each took a few sips and then he put his mug on the side table, took hers from her hand and put the mug next to his own.

"You remember I said we were going to search the prowler's home to look for evidence?"

She wasn't likely to forget any of this in a hurry. "You found something, right? Don't tell me he's going to get away with it."

"He isn't. We've found the photos, Stella."

"Of me?"

"Amongst others."

Stella was glad he'd taken the mug from her hand. If he hadn't she'd have spilt hot tea onto her lap. She ran to the bathroom and retched. After a few moments holding onto the sink, she decided she wasn't going to be sick and returned to the living room.

John was already on his feet and she walked into his arms. She felt safe leaning against him.

"It's OK, we've got him locked up. He'll be in prison for a very long time." John spoke gently, but with confidence.

"Thanks, John," Stella whispered.

John held her tight and told her how clear the evidence was and how all the correct procedures had been followed. "There's no way he can wriggle out of this."

Stella couldn't wriggle out of John's embrace, but then she wasn't trying. What was wrong with her? She was no longer scared, yet she was still trembling.

"OK?" he asked.

"I think so. I will be anyway. It's just that..."

"It's a shock and a horrible thing to have happened to you."

"At least I wasn't hurt like poor Daphne. It could have been worse."

"It was bad enough."

"I'm glad you're here, John. I'm glad it was you who told me."

"I'll always be here for you."

He always had been. Even when they'd been children he'd tried to protect her as well as his little sister. He'd warned off school bullies and later, unsuitable boyfriends. He'd advised on ways of keeping safe and avoiding trouble. He'd also frequently annoyed her when it seemed he was interfering in her life, but deep down she knew he was acting with her best interests in mind.

"Thanks, John. Oh and thanks for the flowers."

"You're welcome."

"And the note. I er, yes. I'd like to do that."

"We could go for a meal this evening, if you like?"

"I can't think about food yet. Let's drink our tea and you can explain again how you caught him and how he won't be able to do this again."

"It's thanks to you we found him, Stella," John said. "We'd had reports of a man lurking around outside the victims' homes. He probably watched them, as he only ever went into places where a woman lived alone and after she'd gone to bed. When he was arrested it was almost by luck. We suspected him, but had no proof, so we couldn't bring him in or search his home. Unfortunately for him, although his last victim usually lived alone, on the night he broke into her home, she had a relative staying."

"The rugby player."

"Yes. He saw the flash from the camera, grabbed the man and sat on him while dialling 999. Your prowler had an asthma attack, so didn't exactly put up a fight while they waited for our team to get there."

"That explains the heavy breathing."

"It does. Once he stopped wheezing, he started coughing. At least, he did when we showed him the photographs of his victims stored on his computer."

"John, the team who arrested him, that was you and Doug, wasn't it?"

"As it happened, it was, but we really were just part of the team. It could easily have been someone else."

"But it wasn't."

John shrugged.

"So he's going to jail and staying there?" Stella asked.

"Yes. There'll be a wait for the court case of course, but he's proved himself dangerous. Other women he photographed have woken up and he's hurt them as he's got away. Daphne was the most seriously hurt, but he knocked out one woman and two others were injured, so we can prove he's potentially dangerous and keep him locked up until the trial."

"Good. That's good."

They finished their tea without speaking again. Stella glanced at John several times, quickly looking away when she saw he was watching her. It was silly for her to feel shy with him. She'd known him for years, dated him for months and rowed with him on numerous occasions. Never before had she had nothing to say to him.

"So do you want to come out for a meal, tonight?" John blurted out.

"Yes, I'd like that. Can you give me half an hour to get ready?"

"Of course. Would you like to go to Trio, or somewhere else?"

"Trio would be great," Stella said.

"I'll go over and book a table and I'll ask Luigi to make us a special beat the burglar cocktail."

"Great. I'll be as quick as I can."

It wasn't until she was in the shower Stella realised that Doug should also be celebrating the arrest and apologising for standing her up. She hoped John was booking a table for two.

"You look great, er not that you didn't before..." John said when he returned. After that he hardly spoke other than to ask what she'd like to drink and order his food.

When the plates of Parma ham and melon were laid before them, John topped up her glass of prosecco. "Do you remember the first time I took you out for a meal?"

"Fish and chips which we ate in the boathouse by the lake. At least, I had fish, you just had chips, as you got to the counter and suddenly remembered you didn't eat fish."

"Actually, I'd realised I couldn't afford two portions of fish as well as your bus fare home."

"Oh! Why didn't you say?"

"I was trying to impress you, wasn't I?"

Stella giggled. "S'pose so. It's hard to think of you doing that now, not that I blame you."

"Why would..."

"Would Sir and Madam like pepper?" Luigi asked.

He held his giant wooden pepper grinder suggestively and they both tried to stifle their laughter as he seasoned their starters with extravagant gestures.

"Do enjoy your meal," Luigi said in his most haughty manner, before mincing away.

They both laughed until they become conscious other diners were staring.

"He's a much better bloke than I gave him credit for," John said.

"I know what you mean. I don't think I really got to know him when I was dating him. The Luigi I knew was like the handsome Italian you see on a film. It was fun, but it wasn't real."

"I think it's the real thing with Daphne."

"Me too. So you're happy about him marrying your sister?"

"As happy as I'll ever be. No man is ever going to be quite good enough for her, but it's not up to me. What about you?"

"It's not up to me either. Despite how I feel, she's not my sister. She's so happy with Luigi though, I'm happy for her. They do seem right together. I'm going to take great pleasure in pointing out how wrong that gypsy was and how right I was."

"So you've got no interest in finding yourself a tall, dark, handsome boyfriend?"

"No, quite the opposite."

She grinned at John. Although he wasn't exactly ugly, John was fairly close to the opposite of that description. "Oh, you mean Doug? We aren't... "

"I know. I should be annoyed with him, but..." He shrugged.

They both turned their attention to the food.

Stella didn't feel as though she could eat, but she made herself chew a small piece. "What were you saying before Luigi came and entertained us?" She asked once she'd managed to swallow.

"Something along the lines of why do you think I don't want to impress you now?"

"Oh." She took a large mouthful of wine. "Maybe because I tried to manipulate you when we were teenagers because I wanted to be part of your family so much, I never stopped to consider what you wanted."

"That was a long time ago, Stella."

"I know, I didn't mean you'd still be holding a grudge over that. You're not as petty as me." She pushed ham around her plate. "After we split up, I wasn't very nice to you. I didn't mean it... it just became a sort of habit and I never saw that I was hurting you and Daphne as well as myself."

"Oh, Stella." John reached out and took her hand.

"Then I used your mate Doug to annoy you and got you on a wild goose chase trying to catch Luigi in criminal activities just because he'd hurt my feelings months before. Oh God, I'm even more petty than I realised. Then I couldn't call you for help when I needed it which resulted in me putting your sister's life in danger."

"Stella, you didn't."

"I didn't hurt her, I know it wasn't all my fault, but if I'd called you instead... "

"Anything else you'd like to confess to, or is breaking my heart, putting Doug in his place, wasting police time and hospitalising Daphne the lot?"

"Pretty much."

"Good, my turn then. After a few dates, I knew you didn't want to go out with me anymore, so when I heard that conversation with you and Daphne, I used it as an excuse to dump you first."

"Oh." He was as stupid and sensitive as her then as she'd been really keen, but hadn't shown it or admitted it to Daphne and her other friends for fear of being teased.

"Sometimes, over the years, I've deliberately said something annoying just to get a reaction from you. I hated it when you ignored me."

"John, I..."

"Let me finish, I haven't got to the bad stuff yet."

"Bad stuff? You're not going to tell me you arranged the blonde in Luigi's flat?"

"No, but I deliberately gave Doug a wrong version of your phone number and, oh yes, I wrote mine in your address book just to let you know I'd seen all those love hearts. Where was I?"

"Doug."

"I might have said something to Gran to encourage her to get us together and it wasn't coincidence that I was right next to you at New Year. Um,.... yeah, I think that's about it."

"You sure? There's nothing about red roses?"

"Ah, yes. Can you ever forgive me for those?"

"I think I'll come up with a way for you to make it up to me." She already had and it carried on from where they'd finished off under the mistletoe.

"Stella, you're blushing."

"Yes well..." She squeezed his hand.

"Do you think the chef will be offended if we ask for the pizza to be boxed up so we can take it back to your place?" John asked.

"No, but she'll be properly annoyed when I refuse to explain why." Stella no longer needed to be told she was blushing, she could feel the heat in her face.

Luigi appeared as though he'd sensed he was needed, or maybe he'd just noticed they weren't eating.

"Luigi, could we take our main course away, we're, er..."

"Going to want to eat it later? I quite understand." He took away their starter plates, but left them the wine.

"You know what, I think he really did understand," John said.

"Oh dear. Still, at least it saves me from explaining to Daphne."

Once back at Stella's flat, she fussed around putting a stopper in the wine and moving the milk so the bottle could stand in the fridge. She wondered about the food, should she try to make space in the fridge for it, or would the oven be the best place. Should she put on some music? Pour them a drink? Would John wonder why she was taking so long or would he know she was worried that this might be her last chance to put things right between them?

The pizza box was quickly abandoned on her tiny kitchen table as John took her hand and pulled her into the living room and his arms. He held her tight and kissed her cheek. Stella wrapped her arms around his back and lifted her face so her lips brushed against his. She couldn't hear anything other than her blood pulsing through her ears. Heat surged through her, caused by the pressure of John's body hard against her and the gentle caress of his mouth as he slowly kissed her.

Eventually, he pushed her a little away from him and cupped her face in his hands.

"Are you sure this is what you want?" he whispered.

"Yes. Are you?"

"I've always been sure."

"Would you like some music?" she asked backing away from him.

"If that's what you want, Stella."

She dropped to her knees and fumbled with the cupboard by the stereo system. It seemed he did understand how nervous she was, because he took the CD from her trembling fingers and slid it into the machine. He reached out his slender fingers, adjusted the switches and soon soft music filled the room.

Almost immediately it was in competition with the ring tone of John's phone.

"Sorry, that's just a text. I'll switch it off."

He flipped open the phone, glanced at the screen and gave a groan.

"Really sorry now and embarrassed, but I have to call him back. It's Doug and he says it's urgent." John tapped the keypad. "What's up mate?... Can't you... I see... Right, soon as I can." He disconnected the call.

"You have to go?" Stella guessed.

"I do. I don't want to, but I have to. Sorry."

"It's OK." It wasn't OK at all, but she could see he wasn't any happier about it than she was. "At least I'll get to eat all the pizza."

"Can I come back tomorrow? I won't be on call then."

"Sure."

He kissed her before he went. Kissed her very nicely, which just made it worse.

"Just you and me then, Thirteen," Stella said and switched on the oven.

Thirteen must have been very thirsty as between them they finished the wine and half of the green liqueur.

Chapter Twenty-Two

Work dragged the next morning. Stella didn't have a hangover, not really, but the April sunshine was very bright and made her squint. It was that which was giving her the headache. Customers took far too long to decide what they wanted, which prevented her from checking if John had sent her a message. The flowers smelt sickly sweet and Pete was irritatingly cheerful.

"Must you whistle all the time?" she snapped when he carried a bucket of sprouting willow twigs into a momentarily empty shop.

"Stella," Mr Clover called before Pete could answer. "Would you mind going to the shop and getting some hot cross buns. I think they might go with our eleven o'clock coffee." He stressed the word cross.

She grabbed her bag and stomped out. If they were going to gang up on her there was no point arguing. Her phone rang on the way to the bakery. It was John.

"Hi, Stella. OK?"

"Yes."

"Good."

"You?" she asked.

"Yes."

"Good."

Marvellous, at least things weren't at all awkward between them.

"Um, is it, um..." John mumbled.

"Yes."

"Yes?"

"If you mean is it OK to come round to my place and bring a take-away to make up for having to rush off yesterday, then yes it's OK, provided you leave your phone in the car."

"Deal. Seven?"

"See you then."

By the time she returned the phone to her bag she was outside the bakery. In the window was a display of cream filled meringues each decorated with mini Easter eggs and fuzzy chicks. She bought three of those as well as a bag of hot cross buns.

Stella walked slowly back to the shop, enjoying the feel of the warm sunshine on her face. It really was a lovely day. Back at Clover's she took a deep breath of the lovely floral perfume and smiled at the sweet old lady who couldn't decide between deep yellow or creamy carnations. Her dilemma was perfectly understandable as both colours were equally pretty. Stella filled the kettle.

"Pete, I've brought cream cakes to cheer me up and apologise for being grumpy. I'll make us a cup of tea if you could let me know when the kettle's boiled?"

"Sure. I'll give you a shout."

"OK, or you could whistle if you prefer."

"I might just do that, lovey." He winked at her.

Stella walked back into the shop and told the old lady she'd just remembered there was a 'buy one, get one free' offer on and she could have both shades. When the customer had gone, she handed Mr Clover the price of the second bunch.

"Thanks for sending me out, I've cooled down," she said.

John arrived exactly on time. His voice over the intercom suggested he felt as nervous as she did.

"Hi," he said as she let him in.

"Hi," she replied.

He kissed her which, due to the plastic bag of hot food he carried, was awkward.

"I've got Chinese, hope that's OK?"

"Did you get lemon chicken?"

"Of course. And Kung Po pork, crispy seaweed and chilli beef."

"Perfect."

They fussed over putting out plates and opening the containers. A couple of times their hands accidentally touched and both of them jumped apart. They grinned at each other, but didn't speak.

"Wine?" John said.

"Please."

The food was delicious, but Stella couldn't eat much of it. She made more progress with the wine. John cleared his plate, but didn't attempt to refill it.

"Shall I put on some music?" Stella said at exactly the same time as John mentioned how quiet it was.

"I'll take that as a yes," she said and went to the stereo.

After selecting a suitable CD, she returned to the table, but only to collect her wine glass. She took her drink to the sofa.

John quickly took the hint and joined her with his own glass and the bottle.

He sat close to her and put his free arm around her waist, pulling her closer still. They didn't speak as they sipped their wine, but this time the silence didn't feel awkward. When her glass was empty, he poured her another half glass and put the bottle down.

"Aren't you having any?"

"I can't if I'm driving."

"True, but you're not planning to drive anywhere for a while are you?"

"No, that's not what I was planning."

"Have a drink then."

"Maybe later." He stood up. "Want to dance?" John held a hand out to Stella. When she took it, he pulled her up and slipped his arms around her waist. They swayed together to the music. Stella's nerves dissolved, but her heart beat just as strongly. She knew he could feel it, as she could feel his beating against her breast.

She brushed her lips gently against his, then dropped her head onto his shoulder, worried that even now she might have misinterpreted his feelings. His hand stroked her cheek, then her chin, tilting her head up. His first kiss was as gentle as hers. More kisses followed; greedy, urgent kisses that she eagerly returned.

Stella wanted to be closer to John, to feel the warmth of his skin against her whole body, not just his lips on hers and his hand on her back where it had crept up inside her top. She undid two buttons on his shirt, but her fingers stopped co-operating when she reached the third. She pulled the sides of his shirt apart to reveal a small triangle of hairy chest and bent her head to kiss the exposed flesh. As she prised undone each button, she kissed his chest and then his belly until she tugged his shirt free from his jeans and knelt to kiss just below his navel.

John sank down next to her. "Seems like a fun game, can anyone join in?"

"No. Just you."

He kissed Stella until she wriggled free.

"Hang on a sec." She tugged the throw off the sofa and covered Thirteen with it. "OK, where were we?"

"I was just about here," John said and kissed her again. His lips and hot, wet tongue left her mouth as he gradually eased the silky material of her top free from her jeans. He pulled her top upwards, stopping to kiss her belly, ribs and breastbone as each fresh inch of bare skin was revealed. When at last he reached her neck, he tugged the top over her head and kissed her mouth. He trailed soft kisses across her cheek to her ear and then, teasingly slowly down her throat. More kisses traced the laced edge of her bra as his mouth moved over the swell of her breasts. He rolled her over so he could drop kisses along her side, down towards her waist. The gentle caress of his mouth tickled. When Stella giggled and squirmed against him, he gently nipped and nibbled her flesh, working his way down towards her hips.

Stella wriggled free, determined to inflict the same exquisite torture on him. She kissed his waist, and ran her nails down his back, just to hear him groan her name. Just as he'd done to her, she edged her kisses lower. His waistband was higher than hers, so she unzipped his jeans and tried to ease the material over his slim hips. He pushed her away.

Before she could wonder why, he'd picked her up and carried her toward the bedroom.

When Stella awoke and saw John's fair head on her pillow, she remembered Daphne staying with her over New Year. Stella been shocked to see what, from the back, looked disturbingly like John lying next to her. Foolishly she'd mentioned that to Daphne who'd teased her. How long ago that seemed.

Stella slipped out of bed and padded, in pink fluffy slippers, to the bathroom. Once she'd dragged a brush over her hair and another across her teeth, she pulled on her dressing gown and made tea for herself and John.

"Here you are," she said as she placed it on the bedside table.

"Morning," he said and grinned at her.

"Morning."

"Come back here," he said, folding back the quilt.

"I can't. Sorry, but I've got to go to work."

"Oh," he stuck out his bottom lip like a petulant child.

She giggled. "Sulking isn't going to help. I'm going to have a shower."

"Can I scrub your back?"

"Tempting, but I have to be at the shop in less than twenty minutes." She rushed to the bathroom before he had the chance to try and change her mind.

"Help yourself to anything in the bathroom and breakfast if you can find anything." She said as she combed her damp hair. "I have to go."

"Give me a kiss at least."

Rashly she moved close enough to peck him on the cheek, which was close enough for him to grab her and pull her onto the bed for a proper kiss. A couple more minutes wouldn't matter, she could run to work.

Stella did run, but she was still late.

"I'm sorry," she called as she dashed into the shop. "I was..." She trailed off and blushed.

"You were doing something you'd rather not tell us about?" Pete guessed.

"Er, well, yes."

Pete and Mr Clover weren't the only people she'd rather not explain to. What was she going to say to Daphne?

John came into the shop at eleven o'clock and asked Mr Clover, "As Stella was late into work this morning, can she make up for it by going to lunch early?"

Mr Clover wasn't taken in by John's dubious logic, but he still agreed to Stella taking an early lunch break.

"We aren't very busy, so you needn't hurry back," he told her quietly.

John took her to the coffee shop and bought them both a sandwich.

"I sent Daphne a text to assure her I was OK, in case she wondered why I didn't come back last night," John said.

"Did you say where you'd been?"

"No, she sent a message back to ask, but I haven't replied."

"Are you going to?" Stella asked.

"That's up to you."

The waitress brought across their sandwiches. Stella grabbed hers and took a huge bite of brown bread, red onion marmalade and hot sausage. Last night's tiny meal, no breakfast and the activity in between had left her extremely hungry.

"Maybe we should keep it quiet for a while? With her leg and the wedding and everything she doesn't need anything else to worry about," she said.

"Do you think she'd be worried?"

"Not about us being together, but... our track record isn't great, is it?"

"I suppose you're right." John sighed.

Stella wished she could swallow her tongue along with her lunch. They both concentrated on their food without looking at each other.

"It wasn't bad, but it could have done with a sprinkle of pepper from Luigi's huge pepper mill," John said.

"Do you think he'll use that at their wedding reception?"

"I wouldn't put it past him."

After that they chatted about the wedding plans in general. John walked her back to Clover's without arranging to see her again.

When Stella got home that evening, the first thing she noticed was the scent from the freesias John had given her. The second thing was the tidiness of her flat. He'd cleared away their meal, putting the food in the fridge and washing the plates and glasses. The throw was back on the sofa and the bed made. Thirteen was sprawled on the rug with a dish of water and a cut out paper fish in front of him. Stella sank down next to him and stroked his silky fur.

"He'll be back," she said. "I'm almost sure he'll be back."

Her phone rang.

"Hi Stella, all right for me to come round?" John asked.

"Of course."

How stupid of her to think he might have been sulking over what she'd said about them breaking up before. He loved her just as much as she loved him. Ten minutes later he arrived and proved to her just how true that was.

Later that evening he said, "Are you sure this time? You weren't before."

Stella started to contradict him. "I, no, you're right, I was scared."

"Of me?"

"No, of losing you. I know it doesn't seem logical."

"It's OK, I think I understand," he whispered in her ear. "We were both just kids then really. We've changed a lot since then."

"For the better?"

"Absolutely."

"So who's going to tell Daphne?" Stella asked after kissing him again.

"She'll work it out for herself, won't she?"

"Under normal circumstances she would, but she can't seem to see anything except wedding cakes and dresses and bouquets. She's totally absorbed in her wedding and so happy I don't want to distract her from it, even though I know she'll be happy for us."

"Then we wait until she gets back from honeymoon? All right, but by then, she'll probably be the only one who doesn't know." He grinned, "Unless the stars inform her otherwise. She always reckons she knows what's going on, it'll be fun to keep this from her for a while."

Stella was kept busy at work. Local businesses now accounted for most of their sales and Stella frequently worked into the evening making up displays for hotel foyers, meeting rooms and corporate gifts.

Mr Clover suggested they advertise for a new employee to work with Pete, but Stella wasn't convinced that was wise.

"Let's wait a while to be sure we stay this busy."

She was just about coping with the work as well as seeing John and spending time with Daphne. With a wedding to plan, Daphne needed Stella, but after the wedding she'd be spending more time with her husband and Stella would want to be kept busy while John worked night shifts.

The planning stage of Daphne and Luigi's wedding occupied all spring and early summer. Luigi made it very clear he thought both girls had marvellous taste and that he'd be delighted to go along with their choices.

There were the dresses to choose and the outfits for the page boys.

"I thought empire line dresses, and suits with mandarin collars for the boys?"

"Sounds lovely," Stella said. It was Daphne's day and Stella would go along with whatever the bride wanted. Stella had heard such horror stories of bridesmaid dresses that anything that wasn't frilly pink chiffon with bat wing sleeves was fine by her.

A menu had to be decided upon.

"Yes," was Stella's response to every single suggestion. Alberto, the chef from Quattro was going to take responsibility, so it would all be delicious.

The cake had to be designed.

"Bigger," was Stella's main input there.

There was a colour theme to select and a seating plan to devise.

Stella had offered to do all the flowers as a wedding gift, but of course even that wasn't straightforward. She made up numerous samples, which she also displayed at wedding fayres to generate more business, and discussed possibilities with Daphne.

Finally, Daphne selected red, white and green colours, to represent Italy.

"No problem," Stella assured her.

"Can I have a sprig of myrtle in my bouquet, I've read that it's traditional."

"It is and you can."

Versions of these conversations were repeated every time Stella and Daphne got together and either before or after each lunchtime shift at Trio when Daphne would pop into Clover's or Stella's flat for a chat. Sometimes they'd even be conducted by text when Stella was at the quiz evenings or whispered during Sunday lunch at Trio.

At one lunch that, or any other form of meaningful communication, was totally impossible. As Luigi and Daphne were honeymooning in Italy he would be unable to leave his businesses before the wedding to visit his family. Realising this, his parents and siblings travelled to England to visit him and meet Daphne prior to the wedding. They were all lovely but being in their presence was totally exhausting. They all spoke at once and were constantly excited. Daphne loved the frenzied atmosphere they generated, just as she loved the chaos of a busy kitchen. Stella enjoyed sharing meals with them, or accompanying them on short outings, but more than a couple of hours made her long for the quiet of the room at the back of Clover's where she prepared flowers in peace.

One afternoon as Stella locked Clover's she found Daphne waiting outside.

"Don't look so worried, Daffs. If the dress has vanished you can wear something else, if the venue's double booked we'll hire a hall somewhere, if it's anything to do..."

"It isn't," Daphne interrupted. "It's nothing to do with the wedding."

"What then?"

"It's John. I'm really sorry, Stella."

"What about him?"

"Look, why don't you come into Trio and I'll explain."

Chapter Twenty-Three

As Stella followed her friend down the High Street towards Trio, she reassured herself it couldn't be anything too serious or Luigi wouldn't have left Daphne walking around town alone. She was even more sure when Luigi greeted her with the offer of a cocktail.

"This one is called 'the good friend' because it is sweet and large enough to share." He placed a huge, liberally decorated, glass in front of Stella. As well as pieces of fruit, umbrellas and plastic flowers around the edge, there were two huge twister straws resting in the peach coloured drink.

"Is that a glass or a flower vase?" she asked. "It's massive."

"Like your generous heart," Luigi said.

"OK, what's going on? I can see you're setting me up for something." They must have guessed about her and John and planned to extract the details of the relationship from her. She supposed she'd have to admit the truth, although if she could she'd hold out until she'd finished her share of the cocktail and maybe a few snacks too. She took a good long slurp from the straw nearest her.

"It's almost summer," Daphne said. "We should do something nice."

"Good idea," Stella said. Drinking a cocktail was nice, and here she was doing it.

"You see, I knew she would be happy to help you," Luigi said with just a touch of smugness. He slithered away, hopefully in search of the perfect items of food to compliment the 'good friend'.

"Er, sorry. What is it you think I've I just agreed to?"

"Doing something nice for John's birthday," Daphne said.

"Us?"

"You really, because I'm not sure I have the time or strength to organise anything else. You two are friends now, aren't you?"

"Absolutely," Stella said just a touch doubtfully. It seemed Daphne hadn't guessed the truth after all. "Sixteenth of June, isn't it? What day of the week is that this year?"

"Sunday. Luigi said he'll make alternative arrangements for the restaurant and help with food and drink, depending on what you want."

"He did?" If Luigi was taking care of the catering then organising some kind of birthday bash shouldn't be too difficult. "Do you have any suggestions?"

By the time Stella, with very little help from Daphne, had finished the cocktail and a plate of parmesan biscuits and stuffed olives they'd decided a barbecue would be fun and had drawn up a list of people to invite.

"Right then, I'll see about inviting people, find somewhere to have it and let Luigi know how many people to cater for."

"How are we going to get John there without letting on?" Daphne asked.

"Leave that to me, I'll think of something." All she need do was tell John she wanted to take him out for his birthday. It was going to be easy just as long as she could think of somewhere to hold the party.

"Thanks, Stells. I really appreciate it and I'm sure John will too."

"Of course he will."

"That just leaves the seating plan," Daphne said.

"At a barbecue?"

"No, silly. The wedding."

"Do you need one?" Stella asked.

"I think so. I want my family and Luigi's to mix, but I don't want people to sit on a table where they don't know anyone and then I have to decide who goes on the top table and what do I do about friends...?"

"I'll be back in a sec."

Stella nipped out to the convenience store opposite and bought Daphne a pencil, stack of paper and a huge rubber.

"Put me next to whoever you like. Good luck with the rest."

Stella rang John's parents to ask them to contact any friends and relatives he would want to be at his birthday barbecue.

"No problem, Stella," his mum said once she'd explained that she had been press ganged into organising the party. "Where are you having it, in the park?"

Of course, that would be perfect! There was even the bandstand area to shelter under if it rained. She'd attended street party type events there, but couldn't remember any food being cooked in the park. "Do they allow barbecues?"

"I don't know, but I do know who to ask. Give me a few minutes and I'll call you back."

Five minutes later Stella's phone rang.

It was Daphne. She sounded upset. "Stella, don't have a go at me but I've just read my horoscope."

Stella sighed. "And what terrible catastrophe is predicted?"

"Well, it's not exactly predicting a disaster, but... It says an unexpected visitor from the past will bring good news."

"That's good isn't it? Or at least it would be if these things weren't complete rubbish and anyway you've stopped taking any notice of them."

"What if I've not invited someone from my past or Luigi's and they turn up just before the wedding and should be invited?"

"You invite them."

"Just like that?"

"Yep."

"Oh. Right. Thanks, Stella."

"Stop panicking, it's going to be a great day."

Compared with keeping Daphne calm enough to organise her wedding, arranging John's party was no trouble at all. In fact, it was no trouble full stop. John's mum rang back to confirm it was fine to hold the party in the park and that she'd take care of the formalities required.

"Dad could bring out something to play music on if you like?"

"That'd be great, thanks."

"No, thank you, Stella. John will be so pleased that you're doing this for him. He's really very fond of you... Well, we all are of course."

"It's OK, really."

Luckily the weather for John's birthday barbecue was hot. Thanks to the large plastic boxes of ice that John's parents provided the wine was chilled. Thanks to Luigi and his staff the food was fabulous and plentiful. Thanks to Doug and Uncle Eric there was music, silly games and reunions. John's friends and family ate drank and laughed all afternoon and long into the evening. And Stella got all the credit for organising such a wonderful party.

"Great job, Stella," Simon from the quiz team said. "With your organisational skills we should make you captain."

"I feel a fraud," Stella told John when he'd moved away to get more food. "I didn't do anything other than make a couple of phone calls."

"Then you obviously called the right people and said the right things. And don't worry, if it'd rained you'd have got the blame."

"I suppose. I still feel a fraud though."

"I feel like a sausage," John told her.

"Have one then, there are still a few of those delish pepperoni things left, I think."

"I meant I feel like I'm a sausage because I keep being grilled. Daphne asked me how we're getting on and then Luigi did the same. Obviously she'd told him to."

"What did you say?"

"Not a lot. Stand by, here comes Gran."

"Just the two people I wanted to see," the old lady said.

"What can we do for you, Gran?" John asked.

"Tell me it's OK to get the feather hat."

"Er, I'm not sure I understand."

"No, I don't suppose you do. Stella will. I saw the two most marvellous hats when I was looking for outfits for Daphne's wedding. One has a huge white peacock feather and the other has flowers. Great big red, pink and white peonies. It's quite amazing."

"It sounds it," John said.

Gran gave him a look, but continued, "I really want to have it, but Daphne's wedding might not be the best wedding to wear it to."

"You think the feather one would be better?" John asked.

"Yes, I do but I really want the flower one."

"Can't you buy both?" John asked. "As far as I can make out that's what you women usually do."

"Buy two wedding hats?"

"Yes, Gran."

Gran squealed. She hugged John, then Stella, then John again. "Remember I'm old and impatient." Then she was gone.

John shook his head. "I can't believe she's that excited over a couple of hats."

"They're wedding hats."

"Yeah, I got that. Daphne keeps looking over at us. Think we'd better mingle or we'll be in for another interrogation."

Long after the sun had lost its heat the guests either left or helped Stella in gathering together the barbecue, picnic tables and food containers and returned them to John's parents' home and Luigi's van. Stella waited until last to be sure no trace of litter remained.

John stayed with her. "I've been thinking about what Gran said about the hats. Two hats would mean two weddings?"

"Yes." Stella felt herself blush as she remembered Gran's hint about the flowers.

"Hmm." He cupped Stella's chin in his warm hand and gently stroked her cheek with his thumb. "She's a little batty at times but she often talks a lot of sense."

On the first of July, Daphne called Stella. "I'm still trying to arrange a date for the wedding practice. It's a nightmare getting everyone together. When did you say you'd be free?"

"Any evening after work between now and the wedding will be fine."

"But what about your new mystery boyfriend, won't you want to see him?"

"Trust me, Daphne, he'll understand."

Daphne rang back five minutes later. "Will you want to sit next to your new boyfriend at the wedding? I could redo the seating plan, what did you say his name..."

"No, don't you dare change that plan!" Stella interrupted. "You want to have fingernails left for the big day, don't you?"

"OK. If you're sure."

"I'm sure. Now stop worrying about me. Have you chosen a day for the practice?"

"It looks like the thirteenth will be the best day. You said it's just a number and not really unlucky, didn't you?"

"I did and it is. Is that date OK with the vicar and Luigi?"

"Yes and John will be free."

"Great. What time do you want me there?"

"About seven?"

"No problem," Stella assured her.

"You make it sound so simple."

"It is. Just tell everyone that's when it will be. Most people will be able to come. Those that can't will just follow our lead. Don't worry, everything will work out just fine."

"I hope so."

"Of course it will, Daffs. The thirteenth is exactly a year since we had our fortunes told. Rosie-Lee said I'd walk down the aisle at your side and that'll come true."

"Yes, but..."

Stella shook her head. How come she was the one quoting Rosie-Lee's prophecy and Daphne was the one sounding sceptical? "No buts. It's perfect timing. Everything will work out just fine."

"You're right. Thanks, Stella."

Daphne did ring Stella a few more times before the practice, but usually it was just to chat or tell her how wonderful the dress looked or about the lovely cards and gifts she and Luigi had been sent by family and friends. Once she'd decided fate was on her side, she stopped worrying and tried to find out about Stella's new boyfriend.

"I can't believe you'd tell John and not me," was a text message Stella discovered one lunch break.

"Told John what???" she typed back before switching her phone to silent. She'd have to find out what he'd said before speaking to Daphne. The next time she would see either of them was at the wedding practice and Daphne wasn't likely to have more than one thing on her mind at that.

The practice was a very informal affair that reassured them all. Even Daphne transformed into a confident and radiantly happy bride-to-be once the minister had patiently explained the entire process and assured her that he'd conducted sixty-eight weddings. Every time he'd said 'or forever remain silent' the guests kept quiet, only once was a ring dropped but that had been quickly retrieved and not even once had lightning destroyed the church halfway through the service.

"I suppose it's normal for a bride to have all these worries?" Daphne asked him.

"Well..."

John came to the minister's rescue. "No it isn't, Sis. Now do you have any sensible questions or can we leave the poor man in peace?"

"No, I think that's everything. Thank you so much."

"You're welcome, my dear."

Outside the church, Daphne and Stella reminded John about the gypsy's letter.

"I hadn't forgotten." He produced the envelope. "Where shall we read it?"

"At Trio?" Luigi suggested.

"Suits me," John said.

"There's not time, we'll be open soon," Daphne pointed out.

"Tomorrow then? I feel it is right I make a special cocktail to celebrate. Without this Rosie-Lee, I would never have met dearest Daphne."

"See you there, then," Stella said.

Chapter Twenty-Four

Luigi's latest cocktail was the same delicate pink Daphne had chosen for the bridesmaid's dresses.

"I thought of the cockney rhyming slang Rosie Lee, so I used chilled Earl Grey tea and rosé wine as the base."

John took a sip and said, "It tastes much better than it sounds."

Stella tried hers. It was light and refreshing.

John placed the gypsy's letter on the table. "Who's going to do the honours?"

"Stella should, the gypsy wrote it for her," Daphne said.

As she lifted the envelope, Stella caught a faint whiff of scent just as she had on the day Rosie-Lee had handed it to her. Then she hadn't known what it reminded her of. That mystery was solved now: it was John's aftershave.

She stared at the envelope. That it smelled that way now was no surprise as he'd held onto it for the last year, but why had she smelled that in the gypsy's caravan? It must be some clever subliminal gimmick of hers. She could remember an incense-like scent when she'd first gone in; perhaps Rosie-Lee arranged for there to be a whole series of smells pumped through in the hope one might trigger a memory?

"Would you like me to read it?" Luigi asked.

She handed it to him.

With a suitably dramatic flourish, Luigi broke the seal and extracted the letter. He read, slowly and clearly. The letter listed everything that Rosie-Lee had foretold; the tall dark man, the life saving, a new job, a daughter, the number three, and two friends walking down the aisle.

"That's right, isn't it, Stella?" Daphne asked.

"As far as I can remember that is pretty much what she said, but it's not exactly accurate, is it?"

"What do you mean?" Daphne asked. "I thought you'd realised it was true."

"Sorry, no. Although I do admit we acted that way when you were in hospital."

John explained about the pair of them getting together to convince Daphne the fortune teller was right so it would help her recovery.

"That's so sweet of you both. I knew you weren't exactly friends then, so it was especially good of you to plan that together. Oh and I suppose you did the same thing when I got stressed over the wedding plans?"

"Afraid so," Stella said.

"I'm not stressed now and even if I get a few last minute nerves, I can distract myself guessing about your new bloke. Don't think I won't work it out."

"I'm sure you're very close to the answer," Luigi said.

Daphne turned to face him. "You know who it is?"

"If your gypsy is right, I do."

Stella resisted the urge to snatch the letter from him. It couldn't possibly be right.

"You still doubt, Stella?" Luigi asked.

"Yes. Maybe it's not all wrong exactly, but it's just guess work. Daphne got a job to do with her senses, but that's pretty vague. You could say the same about lots of jobs."

"Not John's," Daphne said.

"Not unless you count looking for trouble, sniffing out crooks, sticking my nose in..." he said.

"And there's the colour and scent of the flowers I work with," Stella said.

"What about you saving my life? That's not something that happens to everyone," Daphne said.

"True. But I didn't save you, did I? The ambulance crew and the surgeon did that. If anything, it would be more accurate to say you saved mine. If you hadn't come in... who knows what that man might have done."

"Shall I continue?" Luigi asked.

"Yes do. She said she'd prove it was all true," Daphne said.

"*It's exactly a year and a day since I told you both these truths*," Luigi read. "*I knew you, Stella, doubted my every word and Daphne believed completely. I knew that you would try at times to make sure my words didn't come true and at others attempt to ensure they did. That is why I told you each other's fortunes. Stella now has a better job, making use of her senses and the third man she's been involved with will be the lucky one. Daphne is to marry the tall dark man, take a journey across the water and have a daughter who must be told the truth.*

I am pleased for you both that I see much joy in your lives. Lives that will be long, healthy and entwined together."

"She's right, Stella, you have to admit that everything she said is right if you swap them over," Daphne said.

"I don't believe you. You said it was right before, now you're telling me the opposite is true."

"You're both right," John says. "The gypsy didn't get everything right and as Stella says, some of it is open to interpretation."

"Exactly," Stella said.

"But I'm sure you both agree most of what's happened this year is a result of your visit to the fortune teller."

"Exactly," Daphne said, before she pulled a face at Stella.

"No way. I thought she should get a better job even before we saw Rosie-Lee."

"But I wouldn't have applied for it if she hadn't said what she did. There wasn't even a vacancy advertised; you manipulated me into it."

"Me, not the gypsy?"

"You know what I mean."

"Well, yes, I suppose so," Stella admitted. "Daphne, why aren't you drinking your cocktail?"

"Er, um..."

"It is just a precaution," Luigi said.

"Precaution against what? You're not poisoning us, are you, Luigi?"

"No, but there are times when a woman should not drink alcohol."

"Daphne, you're... pregnant?"

"I'm not sure. It might just be the wedding nerves."

"Bet you are. You'll have to tell her she was conceived before the honeymoon. That's what Rosie-Lee meant by telling her the truth."

"So you believe it all at last?" Daphne asked.

Stella shrugged, but nodded too.

"So that means Stella's man is a short, blond, ugly but not strange policeman," John asked as he put his arm around Stella and kissed her cheek.

That was one way of interpreting the prophecy. No one could think of a better one.

"Does that mean...?" Daphne said. "Oh!"

As Daphne said how pleased she was Luigi passed Stella the letter. At the bottom it said, '*Stella, you have your family at last*.' She nodded her head and blinked back tears.

Something outside the restaurant attracted Stella's attention. It seemed to have suddenly got foggy, or perhaps it was just steam coming from the kitchen condensing in the cool air. Before she could decide which was most likely, a gust of wind swirled the mist away and she was looking at their reflection in the window. The thick glass, display menus and Trio's flickering candlelight distorted the image making it seem as though she were looking at an old wedding photograph. Daphne was in the centre; the cream of the menu providing her dress and veil. Luigi was in shadow, darkly handsome in his formal suit. It didn't take much imagination to picture John similarly dressed and to realise he'd look handsome too in his own way. As for herself, there was nothing to suggest a huge meringue of a dress or a flirtatious little veil, but she didn't need to see them to believe they'd one day be hers and that pictures of both weddings would both be safely stored in the same family photo album.

I do hope you enjoyed this book. If you did, I'd very much appreciate a short review on Amazon, Goodreads – or anywhere else.

To learn more about my writing life, hear about new releases and get a free short ebook, news and competitions, sign up to my newsletter – subscribepage.io/ItLSNa or you can find the link on my website patsycollins.co.uk

More books by Patsy Collins

Novels

Paint Me A Picture
Escape To The Country
Firestarter
Leave Nothing But Footprints
Acting Like A Killer

Little Mallow cosy mystery series

Disguised Murder and Community Spirit
in Little Mallow
Dependable Friends and Deceitful Neighbours
in Little Mallow
Deadly Words and Innocent Gossip
in Little Mallow

<u>Short story collections</u>

All That Love Stuff
With Love And Kisses
Lots Of Love
Love Is The Answer

Up The Garden Path
Over The Garden Fence
Through The Garden Gate
In The Garden Air
Beyond The Garden Wall

Keep It In The Family
No Family Secrets
Can't Choose Your Family
Family Feeling
Happy Families

Slightly Spooky Stories I
Slightly Spooky Stories II
Slightly Spooky Stories III
Slightly Spooky Stories IV
Slightly Spooky Stories V

Just A Job
Perfect Timing
A Way With Words
Coffee & Cake
Not A Drop To Drink
Making A Move
Days To Remember
Criminal Intent
Crime In Mind
A Clean Bill Of Health
Your Good Health

<u>Non-Fiction</u>

Form Story Idea to Reader -
An accessible guide to writing fiction co-authored
with Rosemary J. Kind

A Year Of Ideas: 365 sets of writing prompts and
exercises